ALWAYS LOYAL

CUBS FOR RENT #3

CHARITY PARKERSON

Punk
&
Sissy

--Warning: This book is intended for readers over the age of 18.

Copyright © 2019 Charity Parkerson
Editor: Vicky Reese
ISBN: 978-1-946099-60-0
All rights reserved.

INTRODUCTION

Every day Loyal watches him. The desire gets bigger with each passing moment. It's only a matter of time before it explodes.

After an accident left Loyal in a wheelchair, he's spent his days fighting to regain the freedom he's lost. As much as he needs help, Loyal doesn't want to be pitied. When a blast from the past volunteers his time to make Loyal's home wheelchair friendly, Loyal has every intention of staying out of Toby's way. He knows Toby could never forgive him for the past. Loyal never intends to fall back into the same role he played with Toby for years. Life doesn't care about Loyal's good intentions.

Toby has known Loyal most of his adult life. For a long time, he considered Loyal his best friend. There's no way he'll turn his back when Loyal needs him most, even if every second in Loyal's company completely breaks him. Unfortunately, the more time Toby spends with Loyal, the more he can't escape the truth. Loyal will always be the only one for Toby.

As one owner of Cubs for Rent—a business that rents men for dates, home repairs, or simply to keep someone company, Toby has countless men vying for his attention. Loyal is the only one he can't shake. They'll have to face the past and all its secrets if they hope to find their way. Tall order doesn't even begin to describe that endeavor.

ONE

A PAIN HIT Toby in his chest as he watched Tucker and Orion exchange wedding vows. They had—once again—transformed their ballroom for a gorgeous event. This time, it was more personal than the grand opening of Cubs for Rent. Although it was a small gathering of close friends, the place looked great. Toby was happy for Tucker. Plus, he would gain another brother with a few spoken I do's. He was ecstatic Orion had agreed to live here, where Toby could hang on to at least one of his identical brothers. All things considered; he should be over the moon. It was harder than expected to be the one left behind. The way Tanner kept shooting worried looks his way let Toby know he wasn't hiding his mood as well as he liked. He tried harder to smile.

Loyal nudged his knee and Toby glanced his way.

"Are you okay?" Loyal mouthed, proving Tanner obviously wasn't the only one who felt Toby's mood darkening. Toby managed a smile and nodded.

Loyal leaned his way and took his hand. Toby glanced down at their linked fingers. There was a deep and angry red scar across Loyal's hand. Toby's throat tightened a little more. Almost ten months ago, he had lost Loyal's heart. Eight months ago, Loyal had almost lost his life. Toby couldn't think about that wreck, or the phone call he had received from Loyal's dad, Jericho. He had known Toby would show up. Always. There was no one for Toby but Loyal, even if there was no hope Loyal would ever love him again. Toby went back to watching his brother repeating his vows. Nothing killed love like the truth, and Toby couldn't take back Loyal learning his.

As Tucker and Orion shared their first kiss as a married couple, Toby came to his feet. He would make this day special for his brother no matter how he felt. Toby and Tanner both released loud whistles at the same time, making people laugh. They exchanged a smiling glance. It was such a stupid thing, but they had competed as kids, trying to best each other, seeing who could whistle the loudest. Being raised off the grid, in the middle of nowhere, they had been forced to use their imaginations to entertain themselves. Some competitions never ended.

A motion from the corner of his eye caught Toby's attention. Loyal was trying to get back to his wheelchair on his own. Toby swallowed his irritation. He knew Loyal wanted to be independent, but goddamn. Toby was literally inches away. There was no reason for Loyal to risk a fall. He started to help whether Loyal wanted it or not. Before he could move, Loyal settled into his chair. His smile was so luminous and filled with pride when he succeeded that Toby's irritation slipped away. Damn, Loyal was beautiful. His bluish-green eyes were unlike anything Toby had ever seen on anyone else. He had blond hair that had the perfect amount of wave, so it tempted people to touch it to see if it was as soft as it looked. Toby wished he could stop loving him. Life would be so much easier if it would go away.

"I take it you're ready to get to the reception part of this gathering."

An adorable dimple appeared in Loyal's cheek. Just the one. Toby bit back a sigh. It was wrong for

Loyal to be so heart-stoppingly beautiful. "I'm ready for my first drink in almost a year. You have no idea."

With a snort, Toby motioned toward the back of the room where the caterers were waiting for Tucker and Orion. "Let's go. I'm sure they won't deny you a glass of champagne while they cut their cake."

"It's the little things in life," Loyal said over his shoulder as he followed Tucker and Orion back down the aisle.

Loyal's words took Toby's breath. It was the little things. The million and one tiny things Toby came so close to losing when Loyal almost died. Now, he swore, even if Loyal never loved him again, he would savor every second he was given with him. Some things were more important than a broken heart.

TOBY WAS SAD AGAIN TODAY. HE TRIED TO HIDE it, but his unhappiness was an invisible weight on Loyal's chest. It was his fault. Loyal knew that too. He had wondered if seeing his brother marry, leaving him the only single brother, would get under Toby's skin. Toby was gorgeous. He could have anyone he wanted, but he didn't date. Not for pleasure anyhow. He went on nonstop dates for Cubs for Rent, but—as far as Loyal had seen—he made no attempt to meet anyone for real. Loyal was a bastard for how happy that made him. He couldn't help it. For as long as he lived, and probably after he was gone, Loyal would never stop feeling as if Toby belonged to him. He didn't know how to stop feeling this way. Loyal equally didn't know how to get out of the friend zone he was currently stuck in. Of course, after everything he had done, Loyal was exactly where he belonged. It wasn't likely Toby would ever let him in again. Loyal had no one else to blame.

Loyal slowed, waiting on Toby. He patted his knee. "Would you like a lift?" He loved making Toby smile.

Toby shook his head, visibly fighting a laugh. "I'd crush you."

He wheeled back and forth—like performing some crazy disabled mating dance. "Come on, sexy. You should sit on daddy's lap."

The happiness in Toby's eyes eased the pressure in Loyal's chest. "We don't have that far to go. I think these old legs can make it."

Loyal couldn't stop his expression from turning wicked. "Maybe I was just looking for an excuse to play with that gorgeous booty. Oh, well. Sigh." He turned away and wheeled toward the table. Loyal chose a spot out of the way. This was Tucker's day. Even though Tucker had never been anything but nice to him, Loyal counted himself lucky to get invited. If he was one of the Kodiak brothers, Loyal would never speak to him again. They were a forgiving bunch. A wave of sadness washed over Loyal. He fully recognized it wasn't forgiveness. It was pity. There was nothing they could do to him that life hadn't already topped. The thing was, Loyal was pathetic enough he would take their mercy over nothing any day. A lump formed in his throat. His chest and stomach hurt. Maybe he should find a way home. He didn't deserve to be here.

Toby's hands landed on his shoulders. He squeezed. The tightness in his chest eased. Toby bent and touched his lips to the shell of Loyal's ear. "I forgot to tell you, you look gorgeous today."

Loyal's eyes fell closed. He savored the sensation of Toby's lips against his skin. His breath brushing Loyal's ear. Damn. Toby would always be the one.

Tanner's gorgeous husband, Henry, appeared with a glass of champagne. He held it out for Loyal. "I believe I heard you were in need of this."

"Thank you," Loyal said, flashing Henry a smile as he accepted the drink.

Henry tried handing a second glass to Toby. "For you."

Toby waved it off. "No, thank you. I'm driving this one home later."

"If you want a drink, have one," Loyal argued. "I could always stay the night here."

A light touch stroked the back of Loyal's neck, right above his collar. Goosebumps rose on Loyal's skin. "It's all right, sweetie. I don't drink much anymore. But you know you're always welcome to stay the night anytime you want, right?"

"Sure." Loyal took a drink to wash the lie from his tongue. To be honest, he didn't always know where he stood with Toby. For years, they had been best friends. This place had been a second home to him. Nothing was the same now. He imagined, if the day ever came that he walked again, Toby would no longer feel obligated to pretend to be his friend again. Loyal drained his glass. "I'll take that second glass off your hands if Toby isn't interested."

Henry laughed and exchanged Loyal's empty glass for the full one he held. Tanner sidled up beside him and handed Henry a glass. "You forgot to get one for yourself."

Henry looked his husband's way. "I didn't forget. I knew you would bring me one." He sipped the champagne while holding Tanner's stare. Loyal couldn't look away from the heat in Henry's eyes as he ate Tanner alive with his gaze. Loyal wanted to be looked at like that—like he was worshipped. Sometimes, Loyal struggled. He couldn't stop smiling, but he didn't feel it.

Toby stroked his neck again. "Take it easy there, lush," Toby said with a chuckle when Loyal killed the second glass. He leaned down and touched his lips to Loyal's ear again. "I don't really think you want me having to hold you up every time you need to take a piss tonight."

"Oh, I don't know," Loyal said under his breath. "I've had your hand on my dick before. It was pretty amazing."

Toby laughed and kissed his shoulder. "Tart."

Loyal focused on watching Tucker and Orion cut their cake. He didn't ask for another drink. Joking aside, he didn't want anyone to have to hold him up every time he needed to run to the bathroom. No matter how much Loyal flirted, Toby no longer saw him as sexual. The last thing Loyal needed was to give the man even more reason to invalidate him. Loyal swallowed down the bitterness. Life ended for him eight months ago. His body just hadn't realized it yet, but his heart knew

Loyal was dead. One day, he would have to accept it.

———

Toby watched Loyal's mood deteriorate by the hour. The later the night got, the quieter he became, and the less he smiled. He didn't drink anything else after Toby told him to slow down. That made Toby feel guilty enough, considering Loyal got little to no enjoyment out of life as it was, but Loyal also refused everything Toby tried getting him to eat. Toby wanted to scream. Loyal had lost a ton of weight in the past eight months. He needed to regain his strength. Sometimes, it was like Loyal had given up.

The minute the two grooms went upstairs, and guests started to leave, Toby broke. He took control of Loyal's wheelchair and headed for the kitchen. "Come on, babe. Let's find a quiet spot." He stopped in the kitchen only long enough to grab some sandwiches, chips, and sodas. A soft chuckle rumbled from Loyal as Toby dumped the haul in his lap before heading for the back door. He didn't stop moving until they were out on the dock. After setting the brake on Loyal's chair, Toby dropped to his ass at

Loyal's feet. He leaned against Loyal's legs and started dividing the food between them.

"I'm really not hungry." Loyal even sounded sad.

Even though Toby knew Loyal was a warrior, he also knew he was a weary one. "You can't make me eat alone. That's just rude, and I know your daddy raised you better than that."

"I've always thought this was the most beautiful spot in the world," Loyal said, avoiding Toby's claim. He chuckled. "Do you remember that night we went skinny dipping, thinking it would be no big deal since this is your property?"

Toby laughed at the memory. "Like I could forget. We almost went to jail for indecent exposure."

"If I hadn't gone to high school with that one cop, we would have."

To hide his longing, Toby took a bite of his sandwich. That had been the first time he had seen Loyal completely nude. If the water hadn't been freezing, he would have humiliated himself for more reasons than one that night.

Loyal opened the chips. He popped one in his mouth and chewed. While Loyal stared at the water, Toby stared at him. Loyal smiled to himself—like he had a secret. Toby would have paid any amount to hear his thoughts.

"What's that smile all about?"

Loyal's gaze shot to Toby's at the question. His smile grew. "You never would've talked to me again if you had any idea how warm that memory kept me that night."

"I'm not sure there's a single thing you could do that would make me stop talking to you." The memory of Loyal's perfect body floated across Toby's mind. "Especially that," Toby added with a chuckle. Toby didn't give Loyal a chance to respond. He couldn't go down this road. "Have you decided if I'm taking you home or if you're staying the night?"

Loyal ate another chip before answering. "I think I'll just stay the night, if that's okay with you. Dad could probably use the break."

That answered a question Toby had been pondering. He had wondered if Loyal felt like a burden to people. It seemed like—more and more often—Loyal tried doing things by himself that he shouldn't be doing. Toby had questioned whether it was due to needing his independence or fear he was burning everyone out. Maybe it was both. Either way, Toby didn't think it was possible for him to ever get tired of taking care of Loyal. It was his job.

"You can sleep in my room," Toby said, deciding not to broach the topic. "Since I've already added all the safety bars for you in that bathroom."

Loyal didn't speak again right away. Instead, he stared at the water, as if gathering his thoughts. When he finally spoke, the words were hesitant, as if he questioned whether he should say each one. "I know that I don't deserve everything you've done for me. You're still my best friend though. I missed you a lot when I didn't get to see you."

Toby's eyes burned. He knew, eventually, they would have to have a real conversation about everything that happened in the past year. Tonight wasn't that night. They both weren't in their best headspace. All Toby could do was give Loyal the same truth Loyal had given him. "You're still my best friend too. There's nothing I wouldn't do for you." That included letting go of the way Loyal had broken him. Some things were bigger than a past he couldn't change. What Loyal had done, Toby could live with as long as Loyal was alive. If Loyal didn't exist anymore, Toby wouldn't either. He simply wasn't as strong as he liked everyone to believe. His mind was too dark without Loyal's light. He needed Loyal to be happy again. Right now, there was no sunshine in the world.

LOYAL DIDN'T MATCH WITH ANYONE IN THE house. Toby and Tucker were huge guys with broad shoulders and bulging biceps. Orion was tiny and short—like a sprite. Loyal was tall and skinny. No one had clothes that would fit him. Normally, Loyal slept in nothing but underwear. Since he was sleeping in Toby's bed, he felt the need to at least wear one of Toby's huge t-shirts to hide the worst of his scars.

Toby helped him into the bed while Loyal stared at his gorgeous forest green eyes. "I think I need to set up the same handrail system for the bed here as I did for your bedroom." Toby said the words absently, as if more for himself than Loyal.

Loyal fought the hope growing in his chest at the claim. Toby had volunteered his time and the supplies, claiming it was a tax write-off, when he had shown up to make Loyal's dad's house wheelchair friendly. He had put up handrails, built ramps, and basically made their home completely accessible. Loyal had followed him from room to room, watching him the entire time. Toby had no clue how Loyal's heart had been eaten alive every second of those days. Now, Toby was slowly making the same changes to his house. He had already done the bathroom in his bedroom and added a ramp headed to the boat dock. Loyal didn't want to hope that Toby planned to keep him, but he couldn't help it. Toby would always be his greatest love. Loyal hadn't believed Toby would ever forgive him. He still wasn't sure Toby really had. Sometimes, Toby's company still felt like a tax write-off.

"I'm sure I'll be okay. All I have to do is poke you if I need anything." Loyal chuckled. Even he heard the discomfort in the sound.

Toby's face blanked. "Oh. I thought I'd go sleep in one of the guest rooms. That way I don't bother you. If that's okay?"

A hint of panic hit Loyal. He wasn't sure if he could transfer from this bed to his chair. He didn't like feeling helpless. Maybe he should have gone home. "Oh." He eyed his chair. With enough support, Loyal could take a couple of steps, but he wasn't sure he had enough support. Maybe if he leaned on the bedside table. Shit. What if there was a fire? His heartbeat pounded in his ears. What if the nightmares came? Goddamn. He should have gone home.

Toby rubbed his arms, making Loyal wonder if he looked as panicked as he felt. "This bed is big enough for both of us. I should stay. Otherwise, you might jerk off on my sheets."

Loyal punched Toby in the ribs without thought. "Ugh. Don't treat me like I won't jerk off on you if you stay."

Toby roared with laughter as he circled the bed and crawled in beside him. He settled beneath the covers next to Loyal. Loyal measured every breath he took. Toby was so close.

"Oh, shit. Light," Toby said with a chuckle, rolling to turn off the lamp. He rolled back over, facing Loyal. "Good night, sexy."

Loyal smiled into the dark. He wasn't sexy, but he appreciated the compliment. His fingers found Toby's beneath the covers. Loyal's heart skipped a beat as Toby closed his fingers around Loyal's. For several minutes, he stared at the ceiling. He couldn't sleep without speaking a small bit of his mind. "Toby." He whispered Toby's name in case he had fallen asleep.

"Yeah?"

"Thank you for staying."

Toby shifted, moving a little closer. "You don't have to thank me. It's my bed."

Loyal's smile grew. "Then, thank you for sharing it with me."

A full minute passed before Toby said anything else. "Don't thank me for that either. It's always been your bed too."

Loyal doubted that was true, but it warmed his heart, nonetheless. One of these days, Loyal would find a way to be worthy of Toby's friendship again. Somehow.

TWO

A GASP SOUNDED through the air, sending Toby's heart racing into his throat. He had been sitting by the bed, reading for over an hour while waiting for Loyal to wake. Toby didn't want to disturb him, since Loyal didn't usually sleep well. Equally, Toby hadn't wanted to leave him alone in case he woke up and was trapped in bed. A cry followed the gasp, bringing Toby to his feet.

"Are you okay?"

Loyal's face screwed up in pain. "My legs. Oh my god."

Toby rushed to his side and turned back the covers. The muscles in Loyal's legs were all drawn up into tight balls. The pain had to be excruciating. Toby fell back on what they had taught him in the hospital when this happened there, preparing him for when Loyal came home. He hardened his heart against Loyal's screams as he straightened his legs before going to work on the muscles. Tucker stormed the room, obviously scared someone was being murdered. Toby waved him away, hoping to spare Loyal some pride. Loyal covered his face with the pillow while Toby did his best to release the hold his leg cramps had on his muscles before permanent damage was done. Toby's heartbeat pounded in his ears. His chest hurt. Loyal was suffering. Toby had to fix it. He didn't understand how anyone could live like this. His eyes burned. His nose stung. Toby wished this horrible thing had never happened to the other half of his soul. It didn't matter if Loyal never loved him. Toby loved Loyal. Watching him suffer was killing Toby.

Loyal's muscles loosened. His breathing lost a bit of its ragged edge. Toby kicked himself for not forcing Loyal to get enough water to drink and do his exercises before bed. The first night he was entrusted with Loyal's care overnight, Toby had failed.

"I'm sorry," Loyal breathed, sounding weak. "I'm so sorry."

Toby's heart twisted. Loyal was apologizing for inconveniencing Toby with his suffering. Rage and heartache swirled inside Toby. Toby pushed the pillow aside. Loyal looked a wreck. His eyes and nose were red. His bottom lip was swollen and had teeth marks in it. Toby was pretty sure he had almost bitten through it. Loyal had eyes that looked exactly like the waters in Jamaica. They were a bluish green that couldn't be described any other way. At the moment, they stood out twice as much as usual with his flushed face. All Toby could do was stare. In his life, Toby had never met anyone more beautiful. Sometimes, Loyal stole his voice. Looking at him, knocked the wind from Toby.

Toby had to clear his throat to speak. "Just let me know when you're ready to move. Your dad brought you some clothes and toiletries, if you'd like to take a bath. Maybe soaking in some hot water might help."

Loyal swallowed. Toby watched his throat work. Sometimes, it was like loving Loyal was all he knew how to do. "A bath sounds good." Loyal's voice sounded rough.

"I'll get it ready." Toby started to move away.

Loyal reached out, stopping him. For a moment, he held Toby's stare. "Thank you."

Before he could stop himself, Toby dropped a kiss on Loyal's stomach. "Baby, if I know nothing else, I know with every fiber of my being that you would do the same for me. That's who we are. You don't ever have to thank me." He walked away before he said something he couldn't take back—like admitting he would always love Loyal. As much as Toby knew Loyal would take care of him if he was the one in that bed, Toby also knew one other thing beyond all shadow of a doubt. Loyal would never openly love him back.

WAKING UP IN PAIN HAD WRECKED LOYAL'S mood from the first second his eyes opened. Three hours later, nothing had changed. He was trying. Toby was shirtless and working on Loyal's dad's countertops, lowering them so Loyal would have an easier time reaching things. Toby's bare skin was a beautiful sight. He was all muscle and wide shoulders. Every move he made was mesmerizing. Still, Loyal couldn't shake the darkness. He wanted to touch Toby. More than that, Loyal wanted Toby to touch him. His mind itched with the need to see lust growing in Toby's eyes again when he looked at Loyal. Of course, no one really looked at Loyal anymore. It was like people were afraid to meet his gaze—like being wheelchair bound was catching.

Toby bent and scooped his hammer from the floor. Loyal's mouth watered. If only Loyal wasn't such a coward. Maybe he would move closer and stroke the ass that screamed for squeezes. Loyal's heart rate kicked up and not in a good way. Toby might leave if Loyal touched him. What would Loyal do then? He would be alone. Loyal took a breath, staving off a panic attack. Sometimes they struck from nowhere.

"Wow. You've been busy today," Jericho said, strolling inside the kitchen and looking around. He focused on Toby. "I know I've said it a hundred times already, but I can't tell you how much I appreciate all of this. I know Loyal won't be in that chair forever, and he'll eventually move to a place of his own, but this is a huge help now when we need it most."

Loyal headed for the fridge to grab something to drink. If anyone looked too closely at him now, they would see his heart. Once he had a bottle of water tucked in next to his hip, Loyal headed back to the living room. He wasn't needed in the kitchen. In fact, he wasn't needed anywhere. Loyal kept going. His skin felt too tight. He couldn't breathe inside anymore. Loyal headed for the front porch. Once outside, he took a deep breath. Loyal moved as close as he could to the porch railing. After moving his footrests aside, Loyal leaned forward and snagged the wooden railing. It took a few tries, but he finally managed to pull himself up into a standing position. It didn't last long before he had to lean his weight on the railing. His irritation grew, crushing his brain. He missed playing ball, swimming, driving, jogging, and damn near everything he used to do. Now, he was fucking exhausted from standing for half a second.

With a growl, Loyal started to maneuver his way backward. He had forgotten the water bottle and now it sat in the center of his seat. "Goddamn it," Loyal cursed under his breath as he tried reaching for the bottle and holding the rail without falling.

"Whoa. Hold up. I've got it." Toby rushed to his side and moved the bottle from his chair. He grabbed Loyal's arm.

In his frustration, Loyal pulled away, nearly toppling himself. Another growl escaped. "I've got it. You're not always here, you know." Even as he settled back in his chair—winded—his aggravation didn't ebb. Toby's closed expression didn't help. Now, Loyal felt guilty on top of his aggravation. "Sorry. I just have to do things on my own. You won't always be around to help me."

"Sure."

Damn. Toby sounded closed off. Loyal wanted to tear out his hair. He didn't know what was wrong with him today. Loyal focused on fixing his chair. He had to get over whatever this was today. It was like all he ever did was hurt Toby. He tried adjusting his footrests, flipping them back down. It wasn't working out. He had used all his energy by standing. Loyal fought for several minutes, ready to fucking snap. Sometimes, he scared himself. If he finally lost it, Loyal wasn't sure what he would do, and that was terrifying.

"You know what we should do tomorrow," Toby said, obviously trying to calm Loyal's storm before it exploded. "We should spend the day out on the lake again. Except this time, you should drive the boat, and let me relax."

"Sounds good." He liked the idea of bringing Toby some peace. Loyal doubled his efforts to move the footrests without luck.

"Here. Let me, baby." Toby dropped to his haunches at Loyal's feet. "I know you don't want help." Toby glanced up as he led Loyal's foot to the footrest. He stroked Loyal's ankle. "Maybe I need to help."

Loyal didn't know if Toby realized he was stroking Loyal's ankle, but Loyal's heart knew.

"Sometimes it's the little things that send me over the edge. I didn't mean to snap at you."

Toby looked so understanding. So sexy. Before he could stop himself, Loyal touched Toby's cheek. Toby didn't move away. Loyal traced the scar beneath Toby's eye. It was the only feature that set him apart from his brothers. Not that Loyal needed that clue. He could pick Toby from a million clones. "Are you still telling people you got this playing hockey?"

Toby covered Loyal's hand with his. "What else would you have me say? Should I tell people it happened when I killed my dad?"

Without thought, Loyal winced. He wanted to take away Toby's pain, but he didn't know how. He had never known how.

A sad smile touched Toby's lips. "It's okay, gorgeous," Toby said, moving Loyal's hand to his lips. "I don't blame you for not being able to love a murderer. I don't blame you for anything." He kissed Loyal's fingertips.

Words crowded Loyal's throat.

"All right, boys. I've got to head to work."

Loyal pulled his hand away and wheeled back, putting some space between Toby and him. Toby didn't immediately stand. Instead, he dropped his chin and stared at the ground.

Loyal pasted on one of his usual fake smiles while his heart screamed for Toby's touch. "Be careful. I'll see you in the morning."

"Yep. Call if you need anything."

Loyal watched his dad make his way to his truck. Not until he was completely out of sight, did Loyal focus on Toby again. As he looked on, Toby's shoulders expanded on a deep breath and he pushed to his feet. He didn't look Loyal's way. "I guess I had better head home too. You're probably tired of me hanging around and I have a client tonight."

Loyal hated himself in that moment. He wasn't brave like Toby. He didn't... ugh. "Toby."

Toby walked away, ignoring Loyal's plea. Loyal wanted to scream for Toby to look at him. He needed someone to see that he was fucking drowning. Toby didn't slow or look back. Loyal closed his eyes against the sight. He couldn't watch Toby leave, even though it was exactly what Loyal deserved.

IT WAS A NICE NIGHT FOR DECEMBER. NOT THAT

it ever got extremely cold in Austin. There was a hint of crisp in the air, but the stars were bright. The crackling of the fire in the fire pit and the smell of burning wood took Toby back to a childhood he would rather forget. That didn't help his mood after the way things left off with Loyal. This was still better than the football game earlier. Sometimes, it was hard being hired for dates, especially to loud places. The stands had been filled with countless screaming fans. Football was huge in Texas. Everyone turned out to cheer on their local teams. For Toby, he couldn't find joy in anything tonight. He had always secretly believed the reason he had lost Loyal was due to confessing his sins. Loyal pulling away from his touch today confirmed his fears. Loyal couldn't love a murderer. It was too much to ask of anyone, especially someone as beautiful inside and out as Loyal. It was okay. Toby had known he would have to pay the piper for that one act in some way or another. When his father had been found at the bottom of that ravine, it had been widely accepted it was suicide. He had been notoriously crazy, after all. Now, losing Loyal, that was worse than prison... or death.

"Thanks for going to the game with me," Kevin said, pulling Toby from his black thoughts.

"I had fun." It was a lie, but his lack of

enjoyment had nothing to do with Kevin. Plus, he was getting paid to be there. Sometimes, he got the feeling Kevin was just as unenthusiastic about being with Toby as Toby was about being with anyone other than Loyal. He didn't know why Kevin paid anyone to spend time with him. He was young, hot, and rich. Toby could see men fighting to be with him. At the very least, he should have tons of people lined up to go see a football game with him... for free. Toby hated that Kevin chose him. He wasn't what the guy needed. Tucker had always been Kevin's first choice. Now that Tucker didn't accept dates any longer, Kevin had settled on Toby. Toby was nothing like Tucker. Well, they were identical in looks, but that's where things ended. Tucker was fun. He joked and laughed. It was impossible not to smile in his company. Toby wasn't like that. Surely, Kevin felt cheated by getting stuck with Toby.

Despite the fire and it only being fifty-two degrees outside, Kevin's arms were covered in goosebumps. Toby stood and peeled off his jacket. He draped it over Kevin's shoulders.

"Here, I don't get cold easily."

Kevin stuffed his arms in the armholes of the jacket. He flashed Toby a shy smile. "Thank you. I should have grabbed a sweatshirt when we were inside earlier, but I thought the fire would be enough to keep me warm."

Toby waved off his words. "It's no big deal. I'm immune to the elements." He really was. Over ten years of living outdoors had thickened his skin.

"It seems Tucker said something about the three of you being raised off the grid as survivalists."

Even as Toby nodded, he prayed Kevin wouldn't open this topic. He couldn't go down that road. Toby already felt off tonight. He didn't want to talk about his crazy father. The last thing he wanted was to relive the horror of abuse and everything he had done to survive.

"May I ask you a personal question?" Kevin asked, as he stared at the night sky.

Toby mentally prepared himself to talk about the past. "Sure."

Kevin looked his way. "Are you happy? In general, I mean," he asked, clarifying his question.

Toby spent a moment staring at Kevin, adjusting to the change in topic, and trying to decide if he should be honest. Kevin looked like a nice person. The truth popped out. "No. Not in the least." Not since losing Loyal, Toby added in his head.

Kevin nodded and looked away. "Yeah. Me neither. I thought I was getting by for a little while.

It's not feeling so much like I am anymore," Kevin tacked on as if more for himself.

"What changed?" Toby was in his element now, dealing with someone else's problems. He liked helping other people. It made him feel less useless.

Kevin focused on the fire and shrugged. "I saw my ex recently. Honestly, he's a piece of shit and I shouldn't let him steal another drop of happiness from me. Knowing those things and feeling them are two different things. The logical side of me has been done with him for a long time. My heart is just really, really dumb."

Goddamn. Toby one hundred percent understood that one. "I wish I had some advice, but I don't. Not on this one. Sometimes, the heart just wants what it wants, and no amount of good sense will save you. Maybe you're not done." Toby hated to suggest such a thing, since he didn't know anything about this ex. He could be physically abusive for all Toby knew. Not that Kevin didn't look like he could take care of himself. He was a cuddly bear. It hurt Toby's heart to think of anyone being mean to him.

"Oh, I'm done," Kevin said, sounding firm. His voice lost some of his confidence. "I'm just not done with loving him, if that makes sense. Like, I think he was the one, and that really fucking sucks, because he's awful. But I can't and won't go back, so I'm just..." Kevin shrugged.

"Stuck in limbo," Toby supplied.

Kevin nodded. "Waiting on the next life, I suppose," Kevin added, summing up how Toby felt too. He had no shot at Loyal again. Toby was stuck. In limbo. Waiting on the next life.

For several minutes they stared at the fire in silence. Each lost in their self-pity. Kevin broke first. "I'm about to push the absolute limit of your professionalism here, but I have a favor to ask."

Toby nodded. If he could help, he would. "Hit me with it."

"You absolutely can tell me no. No hard feelings. Would it be okay if I kissed you? It's more of an experiment on my part," Kevin quickly added before Toby could answer. "I haven't kissed anyone else since we broke up. Sometimes, I wonder if that's part of my problem. I don't want to lead someone else on and hurt anyone the way I've been hurt, so I don't try anymore. Maybe if I just did it. Got that first kiss with someone else out of the way, then maybe—"

Toby kissed him, cutting off the rambling and taking the choice from Kevin. Maybe Toby needed this too. He poured every ounce of skill into their kiss. If he planned to wreck his sanity by touching someone other than Loyal, Toby had to go all in. He sucked Kevin's bottom lip and nibbled. When Kevin opened for him, Toby completely dominated. He licked and sucked, pushing Loyal away inside his mind. To his surprise, Toby's body reacted. As quickly as the lust washed over him, so too did the self-hatred, because it wasn't Kevin he wanted. It might be Kevin beneath his lips. The way Kevin kissed him back made Toby believe it could be Kevin beneath his body if he tried hard enough. Toby knew the truth though. It wouldn't be. All Toby tasted was Loyal. He could already feel Loyal beneath him. Toby could hear the words Loyal whispered as Toby pushed his way inside. *"My cub. Mine."* Toby tore his mouth away. He rubbed his chest, positive he would find a knife protruding from his heart.

Kevin stood. "I'll take you home."

Toby didn't argue. His tongue didn't work anyhow. The drive was made in complete silence. Toby couldn't even look Kevin's way. When he pulled in Toby's driveway, neither of them moved. For a moment, they sat there in the dark, saying nothing.

Finally, Kevin cleared his throat. "Despite what you might think, I had a nice time tonight."

Toby nodded. "Me too. I'm sorry I'm not more

like Tucker. He's good at lifting people's moods. That gene missed me, I suppose."

"No. Don't apologize. I think I like this better. You don't make me feel like I have to fake it."

A smile hovered on Toby's lips. "You're a good person. I think it's only a matter of time before something amazing happens to you. Most likely, it'll be when you're least expecting it." Toby's smile grew. "Someone as gorgeous as you are doesn't stay single forever. All the rest of the men in the world won't allow it."

Kevin snorted. "We'll see, I guess. I'll see you soon."

Toby nodded. "I'm looking forward to it." With a final wave, Toby slipped from the car and headed for the door. He wondered if he would ever hear from Kevin again. Maybe they had crossed a line that couldn't be uncrossed. Toby wasn't sure how he felt. Mostly, he just felt like he had betrayed Loyal with that kiss. What a fucked-up mess he was.

THREE

TOBY FOUGHT a hard battle with the coffeemaker. No matter what he did, the thing wouldn't brew. He was half a second away from smashing it against the wall. Everything fucking sucked and he was tired of it all. All he wanted was one goddamn cup of coffee. Was that really too much to ask from the universe that never tired of fucking him? The doorbell chimed before Toby managed to have a complete meltdown. Still, he might have stomped a little harder than necessary on his way to the door. It was equally possible he threw the door open with way more force than called upon.

Mister stood on the other side, holding a huge vase of red roses. "Good morning. These were on the porch."

Toby eyed them for a second before relieving Mister of his burden. "Thanks. Come in." Toby twisted the vase until the face of the card showed. They were from a delivery company. "I guess Marie's Floral couldn't be bothered to knock." His gaze dropped to the name. They were for him. His eyebrows snapped together. He headed for the kitchen with Mister in tow. "How are you this morning?"

"Tired, but still kicking. I think I have three parties tonight." Mister dragged out the word "three" like he wasn't sure.

Toby nodded. He got it. Orion hadn't been wrong to think Mister's BDSM demos would be popular. The man had more parties scheduled than one person could handle, but he hadn't started complaining yet. "Yeah. I just finished confirming all of them and I printed out addresses and directions for you." Toby set the flowers on the counter and removed the card.

"Thanks. I don't know my way around Austin that well yet."

"It no problem," Toby said absently as he skimmed the card. *Thank you for last night—Kevin.* "Goddamn it." Toby crossed the room and tossed the card in the trash with more force than necessary. He was so fucking angry with himself he didn't know where to start.

"Is that 'goddamn it' because they're from Loyal or because they aren't?"

Toby ran his fingers through his hair and went back to fighting the coffeemaker. "They're from a client." He dug the heel of his palm in his eye when a pain bloomed there. "I think I really fucked up."

"Oh, shit," Mister said, sitting down hard on the nearest bar stool.

Toby tossed him a glance. "Not that bad of a fuck up, but we kissed, and goddamn it. Why won't this fucking coffeemaker do its damn job?" Toby said, shaking the machine.

Mister closed the distance between them. He gently nudged Toby aside, plugged in the machine, and pushed the button. The sound of brewing filled the air. "Kissing someone isn't the end of the world. Just don't see him again."

"He's already booked me for next weekend."

Mister sucked in a hiss. "That sucks. Now, do you want to tell me what happened with Loyal?"

"What makes you think Loyal has anything to do with anything?"

Mister snorted. "Please. Spare me. You never stop talking about him, and at Tucker's wedding you could cut the sexual tension with a knife. Only love makes people this insane, and this convinced a kiss will end their world."

Toby scrubbed his hands through his hair again, beyond frustrated. "It doesn't matter."

Mister leaned his hip into the counter, looking relaxed. "Tell me what's going on. You never know. I might have advice. If not, you'll probably still feel better for saying it out loud."

Toby blew out a sigh. He crossed his arms over his chest. Fuck it. It wasn't like his love for Loyal was going away. He might as well try. Toby began the only place he could think to start. "Loyal was my first real friend, after my brothers and I moved here. We met when Tanner, Tucker, and I decided to join a local adult softball team. We've always loved the outdoors and are extremely competitive. It sounded like a good time." Toby could still recall every detail of that day like it was yesterday. "I spotted Loyal right away. It's not like I could miss the guy. You've seen him."

Mister nodded. "I have. He's proof of God, for sure."

Mister's description dragged a chuckle from Toby. Loyal was every definition of stunning. "I didn't waste a second. In less than a minute, I was across the field and introducing myself. I wasn't taking any chances he might get away. He was so goddamn kind—like it was unbelievable to me that someone so beautiful was also so gorgeous on the inside too. Then, he introduced me to his very lovely girlfriend." Toby shook his head at the memory. A smile tugged at the corners of his mouth. "I didn't care. I just wanted to be in his company. It didn't matter if we were only ever friends. I adored being with him. It was addictive being the center of his attention—like everyone looked at him and rushed to be near him, but he spent all his time with me. We started doing everything together until we were practically inseparable. He was my best friend, but I'd always been in love with him. Things always went deeper between us. I can't explain it. Then, his girlfriend broke up with him and moved away. I tried not to hope, since I'd never seen him show any interest in a man. But it was like we had this silent agreement. We were in love. We both knew it, and it was real, but we didn't act on it. Mostly, I didn't think I was worth loving, because of my fucked-up childhood. Loyal never made a move, probably because he was more straight than I wanted to accept, but I was so fucked up that his inaction fed my opinion of myself."

A sad smile tugged at Toby's lips. "Then, like a lot of unfortunate stories go, we got plastered one night. We talked for hours. We talked for so long that I was losing my voice. I told him everything. He knew things by the end of that night I hadn't even confessed in years of therapy. I poured everything on him." Toby shook his head. "He didn't even flinch." It was like Toby was there again, sitting in the dark, inches from Loyal. Alcohol or not, he recalled every detail of Loyal. His clothes. His smell. Toby couldn't see anything else. Mister disappeared. He was back in that moment with Loyal. "I don't know who made the first move. It was like we had been inching closer all night until we were sitting thigh to thigh. All I know is the world stopped moving the second our lips met before exploding into color and sound." Toby's stomach muscles tightened at the memory of the way Loyal had looked at him while they made love. He had never seen pure love before that moment. Toby cleared his throat. "The next morning, he was gone. He completely disappeared from my life like I never existed at all." Toby swiped his hands down his thighs, trying to keep his shit together. "I finally worked up the nerve to go to his house a week later after he'd ignored all my calls and texts. That's how I learned from his dad that he had accepted a job in another country. It turns out his girlfriend had never broken up with him. She'd taken a job in Tokyo and they'd been keeping things going long distance. She got him a job at her company. He had known for over a month that he was leaving and never said a word. It was no wonder he didn't flinch hearing about my past, he already planned to walk away from me anyhow."

"How did he end up back here?" Mister asked, reminding Toby he wasn't standing there alone in his pain.

He blinked, coming back to himself. "He only lasted about month before he split from his girlfriend for real. He quietly came back to Austin and I had no idea. Loyal was less than five miles away, and I had no clue. He never tried contacting me."

"Why are you torturing yourself like this for someone who walked away from you without looking back?"

A self-deprecating smile touched Toby's lips. A humorless laugh escaped him. "Because nothing has changed. He's still the one. That was a bit cruel of fate, if you ask me."

"Fate usually is cruel," Mister said, grabbing an empty mug and setting it in front of Toby. He grabbed another for himself and filled their cups. "I met my 'one' years ago too." Mister stared into space, visibly disappearing inside himself. He shook his head, as if shaking off the memories only he could see. A sad smile touched his lips. Toby had to know.

"What happened?"

Mister brought his cup to his lips and sipped, as if washing the taste of the past from his mouth. "I fucked it up," he said, setting the mug down. "He made me believe he would stay and love me through anything. I tested that theory until I broke him." A bitter smile touched Mister's lips. "I'm ridiculously good at twisting beautiful things until they're as ugly as I am on the inside. Some people don't deserve love. I'm one of them."

Toby had a hard time believing it. "Maybe you just needed to learn a lesson about respecting love. Now, you have. You could win him back."

"Oooh, boy. It's obvious you haven't seen how much he hates me. It's okay. We're not talking about me. You still haven't explained why you were assaulting your coffeemaker and kissing other men. It's looked to me like y'all have been working things out lately."

Toby took a breath. He needed to talk to someone, and Mister was listening. On top of that, Mister didn't really know Loyal. The truth wouldn't affect him. Toby turned away and grabbed a nearby kitchen chair. He moved it to the counter and climbed on top. Perched on the edge, he felt around between the cabinets and the twelve-foot ceiling until he found the envelope hidden there. Toby jumped down from the chair and moved back to Mister, holding it out.

"I found this in the mail a few days after Loyal's accident."

Mister's eyebrows rose in obvious curiosity. He set his coffee aside and accepted the envelope. Toby watched as Mister unfolded the letter. His eyes moved from side to side reading the words Toby knew by heart. A few seconds in, he leaned forward and set his elbows on the countertop, as if he could no longer support his entire body weight and the note. Toby got it. It was the heaviest letter he had ever held. Mister covered his mouth and kept reading. The backs of Toby's eyes burned.

After what felt like forever, Mister dropped the note on the counter. His chin lifted but he kept his gaze averted, as if processing what he had read. It got harder to breathe by the second. Toby had been carrying this for months. He should be used to secrets. Toby had his own for years, but this was different.

Finally, Mister focused on him again. He cleared his throat. "Have you talked to Loyal about this?"

Toby shook his head. "He doesn't remember anything about that day. The last thing he remembers is going to a job interview three days before the accident."

Mister blew out a breath. "What do you plan to do?"

With a shrug, Toby pushed the letter around on the countertop. "What I've been doing, I suppose. I'll just keep showing up and watching him until I'm convinced he won't purposely drive another car off a cliff. It's getting harder." Toby's voice broke on the final word, proving how close he was to completely losing his shit. He cleared his throat. "Especially on the days when it's obvious he's fucking done with this life."

"Dude." In one word, Mister summed up everything Toby felt. Some things were just too much. Knowing the man he loved more than life had fully intended to kill himself in that wreck, was one of those too heavy to carry things. Toby didn't know where to go with it. He didn't know how to fix it, especially since Loyal didn't want him to touch him anymore. Goddamn it. The frustration was building again, threatening to take out his knees. Tucker appeared in the doorway, saving Toby.

"Look what someone just left on our front porch," Tucker said, leading Loyal and Jericho into the kitchen. "A set of perfectly good, barely used men. Who abandons something like that?"

Jericho was smiling like he found Tucker hilarious. He was every bit as gorgeous as his son. "Don't you have a honeymoon or something to go on?"

Tucker's smile turned genuine. "We're not headed out until Thursday." They moved to the doorway, chatting about Tucker's plans in Aspen.

Toby's gaze slid Loyal's way. Loyal looked like he expected to get tossed out. "Sorry. I hope it's okay for me to just show up like this. I tried to call but you didn't answer. We had plans to go out on the lake today. You didn't show up." He bit his lip, as if he knew exactly why Toby hadn't come to get him. He obviously expected Toby was finally done with him. As if Toby would ever be done with Loyal.

Horror washed over Toby as he realized he had forgotten all about telling Loyal he would let him drive the boat today. He patted his pockets and eyed the countertops. "Dang. I left my phone in the bedroom. I'm so sorry."

"It's okay," Loyal said, sounding as bright as always.

He flashed Loyal a smile and focused on Jericho now that Tucker had disappeared. "Thank you for bringing Loyal by. I've been working. The morning got away from me when I wasn't looking. I didn't even think about the time."

"Don't worry over it at all," Jericho said, matching his son in smiles. "I was headed in this direction anyhow. An extra stop is nothing, especially after all you've done for us."

Toby noticed Loyal staring at the roses.

Mister snatched up the vase and backed toward the door. "Thank you for intercepting these. The last thing I need is a stalker learning where I live." He laughed. It was an uncomfortable sound. "Anyhow, I guess I had better get to work, boss. Three clients means a full day for me. You can text me the information for tomorrow night's assignments in the morning. If you try to give them to me now, I won't remember any of it."

"Of course," Toby said, more thankful for the rescue than he could express. Loyal might not be his anymore, but he also didn't want to fuck up any shot he might have left.

Jericho eyed Mister. "So, you work for Toby,

huh? What type of services do you provide? You must be good if you're getting roses." The way Jericho laughed had Toby biting the inside of his cheek to hide his humor.

Mister looked his way. His face screamed his unease. It was beyond obvious he didn't know how to respond to someone's father about his work. Jericho waved off his discomfort. "Don't worry. I know all about Toby's business. You can't embarrass me."

A wicked glint entered Mister's eyes, as if a challenge had been issued. "In that case, I'm Mister. May I walk you to your car?"

Jericho shook Mister's hand. "Jericho. I'd like that. You still haven't said what you do."

"I'm a BDSM master," Mister said, leading Jericho to the door.

They walked away without looking back.

"Really? Fascinating," Jericho said as they disappeared through the kitchen doorway.

Toby and Loyal exchanged a knowing glance, before roaring with laughter. Loyal swiped at his eyes. "Why am I imagining my dad peppering Mister with questions for the next half an hour on things he'll never unlearn?"

"Because you know your dad," Toby said, fighting back a smile. He searched for some hint of his earlier irritation and found none. It seemed—no matter what—Loyal would always be his best friend. Some things were incapable of dying. His broken heart and unresolved anger would never eclipse his love. "I'm sorry I'm not ready to go. Mister came by to pick up his schedule and I've been busy setting up appointments and returning calls. I'll run down the hall and change."

Loyal nodded. "It's fine. I've got nothing else going on. Plus, I know you've got a business to run. If you don't have time to go, that's fine. I could always help you get through your workload instead."

"Nope. I promised you a day on the lake. Just sit tight for a second." Plus, he could not disappoint Loyal. That wasn't in him. He would do anything to make Loyal's smiles real. Maybe a day alone together on the water was exactly what they needed. Toby could hope.

TOBY WASN'T PUTTING HIM OUT. THAT WAS ALL Loyal cared about. He had spent the whole night and morning kicking himself for his mood the last time they were together. Then, Toby hadn't answered his calls or texts. Loyal had begun wondering if it was payback for the days when Loyal had done the same. He should have known Toby wasn't bad like him. Toby was good. He didn't hurt people.

Loyal worked up a fake smile. "I'm good to wait as long as you need. Go change."

Toby eyed him for a second, as if questioning Loyal's tone. Loyal tried harder to smile for real. They were together. Soon they would be alone. That's all Loyal wanted.

Obviously mollified, Toby headed down the hall. With nothing to do but wait, Loyal made his way toward the French doors that led out to the boat dock. A movement at the edge of his vision snagged his attention. He caught sight of Orion through an open doorway. Turned sideways, he sat on the couch, reading. As he looked on, Tucker appeared beside him, crawling on his hands and knees. Loyal smiled at the sight. Tucker had always been a ham. In a sneak attack, Tucker snagged Orion around the middle and snatched him from the couch. In a show of flailing arms and legs, Orion squawked. Tucker claimed Orion's mouth, smothering the sound. Loyal tried to look away. His eyes wouldn't budge. Their kiss turned heated—like half a step from clothes falling away. Loyal took a breath. He missed being kissed and touched. No one touched him anymore.

He still had all the same needs and wants he did before the accident, except now no one saw him as sexual.

Loyal finally managed to tear his gaze away. The back door held his attention. He could see the lake shimmering in the distance just beyond the pool. He wheeled toward it. He easily opened the door and made it outside with a little more work. There was no easy way to close the door behind him, so he just left it. The air felt good. Cool. The water was probably freezing. A smile touched his lips as he easily maneuvered the ramps Toby had built specifically for him. Loyal's smile slipped away. Why had Toby bothered? Loyal didn't deserve his kindness. He couldn't understand the mentality behind making it easier for Loyal to get to the dock when Loyal didn't come here often enough to enjoy it. Not to mention, Loyal was the piece of shit who had bolted from Toby's life once upon a time. Nowadays, Toby acted like they had no history together, choosing friendship, while Loyal's love for Toby only grew bigger every day. Some days, he thought he might choke on it.

Loyal moved to the very edge of the dock. He stared at the water, seeing nothing except the images in his head. His body burned with the memories of

Toby overwhelming him. Toby was so goddamn big. He was like being taken down by a bear. A smile touched Loyal's lips. His cub. Loyal's eyes fell closed. He could still see the intense way Toby had stared down at him as he had pushed his way inside Loyal. His muscles tensed. Loyal's lips tingled. He hadn't known a person could physically hurt from missing someone until Toby. That night together haunted Loyal. They had so much promise. If Loyal wasn't a terrible person... if Loyal wasn't a liar. His throat swelled. Toby had been so honest with Loyal. Raw. The reflection of the sunlight shimmered on the water, mesmerizing Loyal. He remembered every second of that night. Toby was ridiculously brave. It was beautiful. Loyal wanted to be brave too. He wanted to be whole. It was unfair for Loyal to be here. He shouldn't be here. Loyal shouldn't be anywhere.

***

LOYAL WASN'T WHERE TOBY LEFT HIM. THE moment he stepped into the hall he spotted the open back door. Toby headed outside. After casting a quick glance around the backyard, Toby caught sight of him on the dock. Something felt off in his gut.

49

Loyal hadn't been himself the past few days. It was obvious the strain of coming home and struggling to adjust was wearing him down. He was at everyone's mercy and it chafed. It seemed like every minute, he felt Loyal's unhappiness grow.

The moment he was within earshot, Toby spoke up. Loyal was too close to the edge of the water for Toby's peace of mind. "Hey, gorgeous. Why didn't you wait for me?"

Loyal didn't respond or look his way. Instead, he turned his face toward the sun. Toby picked up the pace. He swore he felt Loyal's intentions a half second before it happened. Loyal pushed from the chair, falling headfirst into the water. Shock froze Toby's feet to the ground for a heartbeat before he flew into action. He ran full speed for the dock. Toby didn't stop to think. He simply dove in, shoes and all. Nothing mattered but saving Loyal. Loyal surfaced as Toby did. Rage owned Toby as he spotted Loyal, leisurely swimming his way, obviously keeping himself afloat by cutting through the water with his arms. Toby snagged him around the waist. Despite being six inches from Loyal's face, Toby screamed at the top of his lungs in his anger and fear. "What the fuck are you doing? Are you trying to kill yourself?"

Loyal's arms encircled his neck. "I knew I wouldn't drown." His teeth chattered on the words.

The cold cut through Toby's rage. He took a breath. "You scared the shit out of me. I already lost five years of my life when you had your wreck. Are you hoping to kill me? Is that what this is?" He headed toward the shore, while holding tight to Loyal. Toby needed to get Loyal to the house before they died of hypothermia. The water was probably close to fifty degrees, but it was the way the cool water dropped the body temperature that mattered. With Loyal's already compromised nerve sensation there could be any number of problems. Toby was so furious he couldn't think straight. It was like Loyal didn't realize it would kill Toby if he died.

He fought his way out of the water, holding Loyal. The weight of their clothes coupled with the weight of knowing Loyal had just purposely leapt into the lake nearly buckled Toby's knees. His eyes burned as he headed for the house. He couldn't even look at Loyal. Toby couldn't help him. He didn't know how to help him.

Every step he took was filled with rage.

"I'm sorry, Toby. Take me back to my chair. I'll go home."

"Shut the fuck up, Loyal."

Tucker came running, meeting him halfway. "What the fuck? Are you two okay? What happened?"

Toby pried his back teeth apart. "Would you bring Loyal's chair inside? I need to get him warm."

"Yeah. No problem." Tucker looked between them, as if scared to leave them alone.

Toby didn't slow.

Loyal sniffed.

An animalistic growl rose in Toby's throat, choking him. He fought the urge to look.

"I want to go home now."

Toby ground his back teeth. He stomped his way down the hall, ignoring Loyal's pitiful sounding claim. When he reached his bedroom, he headed straight for the bathroom. Toby set Loyal on the edge of the tub, leaving him to cling to the grab rail, while he moved to turn on the shower. He checked the water temperature before moving back to help Loyal. Not once did he meet Loyal's stare. He couldn't. Toby was half a second away from completely losing his shit. He tugged off Loyal's shoes.

"Please just stop. I don't need your help."

Something inside Toby broke. His gaze jumped to Loyal's face. Tears streamed down Loyal's face unchecked. Everything snapped. "Stop fucking running away from me." The yell bounced off the walls, assaulting Toby's ears. Loyal flinched but it was too late. He couldn't take anymore. Toby hadn't gotten his say when Loyal skipped town. He had been forced to hold his tongue after Loyal drove off a cliff. Toby was sick from choking on all the words. "Stop trying to leave me. Goddamn, Loyal. Tell me you hate me, for fuck's sake. Say it makes you sick that you let someone capable of killing their own father touch you. I don't care anymore. Tell me you can't stand knowing that I made love to you without letting you sober up after telling you about the twisted things I'd been forced to do as a child. But for fuck's sake, stop trying to die to get away from me." Toby choked on the words. He couldn't do this anymore. Toby was blind with rage.

Loyal cupped his face. Reality snapped back into focus. He realized the reason he couldn't see was because he was crying too hard. Loyal's unbelievably gorgeous eyes became his anchor. He had dreamed about those eyes since the first day they met. Loyal looked completely calm for someone on the receiving end of Toby's fury. He stroked Toby's face.

"Is that really what you think? You think I want to die to get away from you?" Loyal swiped away Toby's tears with his thumbs. "Baby, you're the only reason I still get up every day." A deep pain that took Toby's breath settled into Loyal's eyes. "But maybe I died, and no one told me. That would explain why everyone acts like they can't touch me. They act like I'm helpless." He visibly swallowed. A tear trailed down his cheek. "Maybe this is hell, having to live in a wheelchair while everyone acts like I'm not—" Loyal dragged his hand through his hair and growled. "Never mind. Nobody ever hears me. Nobody ever has."

Toby could barely breathe. "Everyone acts like you're not what?"

More tears spilled over Loyal's lashes. He made no move to wipe them away. Instead, he stayed focused on dragging his thumb across Toby's bottom lip. When Loyal finally responded, his voice was barely above a whisper. "Like I'm no longer a man. It's harder coming from you than anyone. I don't hate you. You don't make me sick." Loyal's voice grew stronger. "Please don't ever say those things to me again. I love you." His hand fell away. He held tighter to the railing Toby had installed in his bathroom just for Loyal. That was how much he loved him. Toby wanted to rearrange everything in his entire world to make life easier for Loyal. Loyal was back to not looking at him. He sniffed. His chest expanded as he took a deep breath. "You should probably get warmed up. I can barely feel anything anyhow, so don't worry about me."

On his knees at Loyal's feet, Toby stared at Loyal in a haze of crippling heartbreak. Whatever thin veneer kept him held together fell apart. Toby wrapped his arms around Loyal's waist, pressed his face to his stomach and held on. He couldn't be the caretaker anymore. Everything hurt. He was broken. Toby didn't know how to keep going like this. He was so mentally tired he couldn't pull himself off his knees.

Loyal ran his fingers through Toby's hair. Toby held on for dear life. Truthfully, he was keeping Loyal from falling into the floor as much as he was using Loyal to hold himself together. Without thought, Toby's lips brushed Loyal's stomach. His fingers found their way beneath the back of Loyal's shirt. The material moved higher until Toby's lips brushed bare skin. His lips moved higher. Toby kissed the scar above Loyal's collarbone as he peeled the shirt over Loyal's head. He kept going until he could lick Loyal's pulse point. Toby heard Loyal take a ragged breath. He shot to his feet. The flash of pain he caught crossing Loyal's features was almost his undoing. Toby rushed to make it right. He quickly shut down the shower, peeled off his shirt, and returned to Loyal's side. Loyal stared up at him with flushed cheeks and lust in his eyes. Goddamn. He had missed that look from Loyal. Toby swept the man into his arms and headed for the bed. He didn't care if Loyal's wet pants ruined his bedding. They wouldn't for long and he planned to do worse things to his sheets.

After settling Loyal on the bed, Toby immediately started peeling away what was left of his clothes. Loyal didn't try to stop him, but some of the desire drained from his face. There were so many scars. Goddamn. Toby's chest hurt. His beautiful angel had gone through so much.

Loyal stared down the line of his body. "My outside looks like I do on the inside now."

Then they matched. "You look like my beautiful warrior."

Loyal's gaze met his. "I don't really know how this will go. I don't want to disappoint you."

Toby held Loyal's stare as he worked on getting out of his wet clothes. "Baby, as long as I have you beneath me and I can taste your lips, I'm the happiest man on earth. You have no idea how much I've missed you being right there." That was no exaggeration. This was their bed. Maybe they had only had one night together but this was their room. This was the home he wanted to share with Loyal. Loyal was the most beautiful man in the world to Toby. If he had ever seen anyone who matched Loyal, Toby couldn't recall it. No one else was good enough to fill his spot in Toby's heart.

Right now, Loyal looked a nervous mess—like he expected Toby would change his mind and reject him, or his body would fail him and then so would Toby. Toby crawled onto the bed. The only way Loyal could ever fail him would be for him to quit on him again. There would never be anyone else for Toby. Toby needed him to fight for once.

His gaze landed on a small tattoo on Loyal's hip. He didn't know how he missed it while stripping away Loyal's clothes. Toby traced the words with his fingertip. His brain couldn't absorb what his eyes showed him. It was a small bear paw along with the words *My Cub*. His gaze moved to Loyal's. Loyal stared back unashamed.

Toby pressed his lips to the tattoo. Goddamn. He was in love with Loyal. It trashed his heart, seeing proof Loyal loved him too. Loyal's skin was ice cold beneath his lips, reminding Toby he still needed to warm him. Toby snagged the covers and straddled Loyal's body. He sucked in a hiss as his body collided with Loyal's. As much as he wanted to make love to Loyal, his heart demanded he protect Loyal's health. Toby draped himself and the covers over them, creating a cocoon.

"Toby?"

"Yes, baby?"

"Are you ever going to kiss me?"

Toby couldn't explain exactly what was going on in his head. That tattoo. This was his man. His heart. "I need to make sure you're taken care of. My heart needs you to be safe."

A sweet smile touched Loyal's lips. "If you want me warm, you should kiss me. Nothing gets me hotter faster than your kiss."

He didn't need to hear anything else. Toby touched his lips to Loyal's. It was like time fell away. Everything bad that had happened since the last time they kissed ceased to exist. There was nothing but Loyal's mouth opening beneath his. Their tongues brushed. Toby was stricken so hard by desire, he nearly came without warning. His entire body tensed with anticipation. Love crashed over him. Toby deepened their kiss, desperately trying to get even closer. They were one soul and Toby needed to sew them back together.

Loyal's hands moved from Toby's hips to his ass.

He pulled Toby closer. Toby's hips automatically rocked forward. His erection brushed Loyal's. A moan vibrated from Loyal's throat and surrounded Toby's tongue. Toby's heart sped. His skin tightened. It was Loyal beneath him—the man his body had burned for, for longer than he could recall. Toby couldn't stop thrusting against him, using Loyal's erection against his like a masturbation toy, except his heart knew he was making love to the love of his life. Toby's eyes burned with unshed tears.

"I've missed you," Toby whispered between kisses. "I've fucking missed you so much." He lost control as his heart completely took over. Toby nipped at Loyal's jaw and moved to his neck. He sucked as he reached between them and stroked. Toby held their cocks together and thrust.

Loyal gasped. "Oh, god. Toby."

Hearing his name on Loyal's lips in just that tone nearly sent Toby over the edge. He had to suck several deep breaths to keep from coming right then.

"I want you inside me."

Toby froze at the words. "Are you sure?" Not only had it been a long time for Loyal, it had only been that one time for Loyal. That night, he had spent hours toying with Loyal's body, getting him ready. Toby didn't have hours of patience in him today.

"Please, Toby."

At the plea, Toby broke. He wouldn't make his baby suffer, but his heart had needs too. "First, you come for me, and then I'll fuck you."

"Jesus," Loyal breathed, sounding two steps beyond turned on as Toby kissed his way down Loyal's body. He paused at Loyal's tattoo and spent a moment paying homage to the mark that proved Toby hadn't waited for Loyal in vain. Love swelled in Toby's chest, stealing his breath. He swallowed Loyal's cock without mercy. Toby didn't tease. As much as he needed Loyal's cum on his tongue, his man had asked him to fuck him. Toby needed Loyal to fly before his body decided not to wait until it was inside Loyal.

Toby used his saliva to finger Loyal's asshole. He probed and stretched while massaging Loyal's prostate. Loyal's moans caressed Toby's ears while Loyal scratched at the covers and Toby's shoulders. When Loyal came he cried Toby's name and Toby nearly joined him over the edge at the sound. No one knew. No one understood how he had waited, prayed, and pled with any god listening to bring this man back to him. Here he was, flying apart inside Toby's mouth. Toby was the one making him beg.

He kissed a slow path up Loyal's body. Even though Toby was on fire, he needed to savor this. Loyal had already proven that he might run afterward. Toby had to drag this out. When he reached Loyal's mouth, Toby kissed him deep, pouring his love and desire into every stroke. Toby reluctantly moved away long enough to grab some lube. Then, he was right back to worshiping Loyal's lips.

With his fingers coated, Toby ensured his dick and Loyal's asshole were as slick as possible. He didn't want to hurt Loyal. This was all about the pleasure. As Toby pushed his way inside and Loyal begged for more, it hit Toby. He hadn't thought about a condom at all, because it was Loyal. Not only did the guy completely wreck Toby's brain, they were meant to be just like this. They belonged to each other. Toby didn't touch other people, and he knew in his heart Loyal didn't either. The heat of Loyal's body and the way he tried sucking Toby deeper took over Toby's every thought. He couldn't focus on anything else. Toby rocked forward while his tongue moved against Loyal's. Loyal made tiny mewling sounds that vibrated through their kiss.

Toby was completely focused on the man beneath him and the pleasure he brought. His balls were already drawn up tight. Toby tried going slow, making love to Loyal. Loyal felt too good. It had been way too long. Ten months to be exact. Fuck. Had it only been ten months? Those months felt like forever. Loyal had left him, moved away, moved back, wrecked, and spent months in the hospital before ending up right back here with Toby. It was insane how life worked. A ripple of ecstasy tightened his muscles and reminded Toby his attempts at distracting himself weren't working.

"Fuck, Loyal. I'm not going to last. You feel too good. I'm about to come."

"I want it," Loyal begged, sounding desperate.

That was all the permission Toby needed. The spring winding tight inside Toby snapped. "Oh, shit. Loyal. Goddamn. I love you." Words continued flowing from Toby with no real logic behind them. Toby's body was in control. He shook and gasped as he pumped Loyal's ass full of cum. His dick twitched with aftershocks. He was a complete mess mentally and physically as he rolled to his side to keep from crushing Loyal with his massive weight. His mind raced with a million thoughts as his body vibrated in the aftermath of ecstasy. Every thought in his head came back to one place—he would never let Loyal leave him again. Never.

LOYAL STARED AT THE CEILING AND GASPED FOR air. Just as the last time they had made love, Loyal's mind was completely blown. He hadn't forgotten a thing. Loyal wondered sometimes if he had built Toby up in his mind. He hadn't. Toby was every bit as amazing as Loyal remembered.

"Damn."

Toby chuckled and crawled closer. His mouth covered Loyal's. Loyal didn't want Toby to ever stop kissing him. He was so in love with this man. Everything about him. Loyal buried his fingers in Toby's hair. He even loved the sensation of Toby's soft locks slipping through his fingers. Before Loyal met Toby, he hadn't known anyone could be so completely enamored by every aspect of someone. Loyal had never been able to control it.

"So in love with you," Loyal whispered between kisses.

With a final nibble on Loyal's bottom lip, Toby curled around Loyal's body and held on. It was like he was afraid to let go.

Loyal toyed with Toby's hair. "Are you okay, angel?"

"I'm scared to go to sleep."

He kissed Toby's chin. "Why? You can talk to me, baby."

Toby tightened his hold on Loyal. "The last time we made love, you left the country to get away from me."

A growl burst from Loyal without his permission. "I wasn't trying to get away from you."

For a long moment, silence grew between them. When Toby finally spoke, he sounded hesitant. "I think I really need to know, why did you lie to me about Cameron?"

Toby deserved answers, even if Loyal didn't fully understand either. "I think I was lying to myself as much as I was to you. When Cameron left for Tokyo, I kept telling myself I would never see her again. Maybe agreeing to do the long-distance thing was just a way for us to break up without hurting each other, but she would meet someone else—like I wanted to believe we were over. Then she found me that fucking job." Loyal shook his head. "I kept thinking it wasn't real. The thought of leaving you behind was a constant knife in my heart and throat. Every time I tried to tell you, I couldn't." Loyal swallowed. "I couldn't say goodbye to you. Literally, my lips wouldn't form the words, but I was equally terrified of saying I wanted to be with you. My whole life, I've only dated women. I was so goddamn scared, Toby. Then, I got there, and nothing was right. Cameron was overjoyed to have me there while I just felt sick all the time. Everything felt like a lie. Every time she tried getting intimate, I couldn't do it—like literally couldn't. My body stopped working. At first, I blew it off as being tired from traveling and adjusting to the time difference." Loyal shrugged. "But after a while, that didn't fly. She was confused and hurt. Then, she was bitter and angry. She wasn't wrong. I was in love with you and she didn't deserve to have me weighing her down because I was too chicken shit to say I wanted you." Loyal stared at the ceiling. "I failed everyone. That hasn't really changed, I guess."

"That's not—"

"Do you know my dad asked about you damn near every day when I got home?" Loyal said, cutting Toby off before he could lie. He knew better than to think for a second, he wasn't letting everyone down every day. "He would ask why you didn't come around or what you were up to now. I would just make shit up about how busy you were or pass along what news I'd gotten secondhand. One day, I ran in to Tucker at the gas station, he told me about Cubs for Rent. I told Dad—like I'd heard it from you. It was like I stopped knowing how to tell the truth." Loyal turned his head and met Toby's stare. "It's always only been you. I'm so sorry." Loyal's voice gave out on the apology. He had fucked up. Since the night he sneaked away, Loyal hadn't stopped screwing up. He had ruined everything, including his future. It was a hard pill to swallow.

Toby kissed him at the exact moment Loyal almost cracked open and fell apart, saving him. Toby always came to the rescue. His tongue stroked Loyal's, taking away the pain. That's what being with Toby was like for him—finding peace where there was none. Toby was his protector. His cub.

FOUR

AN ALERT on Toby's phone startled him awake. He checked the face. It was a reminder about Loyal's afternoon therapy session. Seeing Loyal's name on his phone had Toby quickly rolling. Loyal's side of the bed was empty. His heartbeat pounded in his ears. He didn't understand how Loyal had even gotten away, much less made a break for it quietly enough not to disturb Toby.

Toby jumped from the bed and stormed the door. He had it open before he remembered he was nude. With a growl, Toby slammed the door and went in search of some shorts. Needing to pee slowed him even further. By the time he made it to the kitchen, Toby's blood pressure was through the roof. He found Loyal struggling to get the coffee container from the cabinet.

A wave of relief nearly buckled his knees. Toby closed the distance between them and snagged the coffee even as he wrapped one arm around Loyal's waist for support. He could feel the way Loyal shook from the exertion.

"Good morning, sexy. How did you manage to sneak away?"

Loyal flashed him a grateful smile as Toby eased him back down in his chair. "Tucker brought my chair in this morning, worried I would need it. I had him help me up so you could sleep."

Despite his best efforts, a tick started behind his eye. "You were nude." He didn't mean to sound so jealous. It was Tucker. There was no pride or secrets between the brothers. They had seen, done, and been through everything together. But Loyal was sacred to Toby.

Loyal chuckled at Toby's open jealousy. "Don't worry. It seems, after my last stay with no extra clothes, Orion bought me some t-shirts and shorts." He motioned at the red shirt and black shorts he wore. "I shimmied on some shorts beneath the covers and then Tucker helped me to my chair."

With every word Loyal spoke, Toby's pride grew.

"That was really amazing of Orion. I'll have to repay the favor."

"He's a good person," Loyal said, sounding moved. "He said he understood what it was like to have nothing to wear, or eat for that matter. I get the impression he didn't have a happy childhood."

Toby nodded. "He was an orphan. I haven't gotten my kiss this morning."

"You haven't tried," Loyal shot back.

Barely fighting a huge smile, Toby bent and brushed his lips across Loyal's. "I'll make the coffee. You sit there and look sexy."

Loyal flashed him a quick grin and backed out of the way.

Toby spoke over his shoulder as he got the coffeemaker ready to brew. "After breakfast, I'll run you home—if you'd like—so you can do whatever you need before I take you to therapy this afternoon."

Loyal nodded along. "Sounds good. I thought—if you don't mind—I would stay again tonight. Orion asked me to go Christmas shopping with him tomorrow while Tucker is at some charity event checking up on a complaint y'all got about a handsy client. I'd like to go. I get that it's a lot of work for anyone to take me anywhere. It was nice of Orion to invite me. I don't want to make it harder on him by having to pick me up too."

Toby hated that Loyal felt like being his friend was a chore. "Orion wouldn't have asked if he thought it would be a burden, but you also don't need an excuse to stay the night. I always want you here. You need to learn you're not putting anyone out. We love you. You're part of this family, unwilling participant or not. We will drag you kicking and screaming along for the ride. Okay?"

The way Loyal tried hiding his smile was adorable. He was happy today. Genuinely. It felt right—like they were finally headed down the path meant for them. Toby needed things to stay this way. His life had been too hard. Everything was always a challenge for him. Toby needed his relationship with Loyal to be a soft landing instead of the ass kicking it had been before yesterday.

"What?"

Loyal's question made Toby realize he had been standing there, staring at Loyal without saying anything for longer than was comfortable for Loyal. Toby took a deep breath, stretching out the staring contest for a few seconds longer. "I'm not sure I've ever told you that you're the most beautiful man I've ever set eyes on. The first moment I saw you, I was lost. No one else on the planet measures up to you in my eyes. No one could ever take your place."

Loyal looked as if he hung on every word, and Toby knew he should have said them sooner. He visibly swallowed. "Same." Loyal cleared his throat and looked away, making Toby realize he was being too intense again. Before he could sweep aside the topic, Loyal spoke up, but he still didn't look Toby's way. "I woke up thinking about how I should've made you breakfast last time, instead of leaving. I should have come in here and cooked for you. There's a lot I should've done differently. I thought—maybe—I could make it up to you today, but it wasn't as easy as I hoped. My mind still thinks I can do things my body won't do."

Fuck. He loved this man. "You know what I think is better than you making me breakfast? Is making breakfast together," Toby said, refusing to make Loyal play a guessing game. "I think that makes us realer—like a genuine couple who shares the workload."

Loyal's gaze had locked onto Toby halfway through his speech. He hadn't looked away since. Toby knew he felt the same. They were real. This was permanent. They would fight for each other now. Neither of them would accept anything less.

TOBY LOOKED HOPEFUL—LIKE HE REALLY believed in Loyal. Loyal would have given him anything in that moment. "Coffee first," Loyal said, ready to do whatever it took to make Toby see they were real.

Toby tossed a glance toward the coffeepot. "It's done. Grab a mug and I'll get the sugar."

With a nod, Loyal pushed his chair as close to the counter as he could. He snagged the grab bar Toby had installed and pulled himself up to stand at the counter. As he reached for a coffee cup that was turned upside down next to the sink, Loyal's gaze landed on an open letter on the counter. His signature stared up at him. Loyal's hand shook as he picked it up. His ass hit the chair. Loyal couldn't believe he didn't hit the floor instead. It always took every ounce of his strength and focus to be upright for any length of time. His brain stopped working at the sight of the note.

Loyal's gaze moved over the words, taking them in.

TOBY,

I have so much to say. Too much for a letter. Even more than you'd be willing to hear, I'm sure. It's a lot harder to smile than it used to be. But I can't stop trying to fake happiness. My therapist says it's kind of like being anorexic. When people have eating disorders, they tend to cook a lot for other people, so they can watch them eat. In a way, that makes sense. I always loved watching you smile. You have no idea how much I miss you. It's cement boots, dragging me down while I'm already drowning.

I'm so tired. Maybe I won't even send this letter. I don't know. I guess I just feel like I've already left you with too many unanswered questions. Then again, maybe I'm a selfish bastard to the end and I just want one more conversation with you. Even if it's only one sided, I still feel closer to you just writing these words. It's gotten to be too hard, knowing I'll never hear your voice again.

Dad asked about you again today. I smiled and said you'd told me to tell him hi. Sorry about that. I'm not strong enough to tell him the truth and that you hate me now. So, I imagine you'll be the first person he calls when I'm gone. Sorry about that too. I've never been good at goodbyes. In truth, I've never really been good at anything, especially living. Honestly, I've never been very attached to it. There was this one night that life felt perfect though. Unfortunately, reality waited for me in the morning, reminding me of all the truths I hadn't shared with you. All the truth I hadn't shared anywhere. You opened your heart and gave me everything while I choked on my words. Another fake smile. Another mask. I'm sorry I took so much more than I gave. It's my biggest hope that you're living your best life and that you think of me every now and then and smile. When Dad calls, please don't tell him about this note. He's suffered enough loss because of me without finding out I'm not who he thought. I just needed to say something to you that I should have said a long time ago, and I won't get a chance after tonight. I love you. You were the one for me. I haven't touched anyone else since that night with you. My stomach churns at the thought of anyone else's hands on my body. Thank you for sharing a piece of your life with me. Maybe, if there is an afterlife, I'll see you on the other side. I pray you can love me there. It's too hard to think I'll never hold you again. So, I'll tell myself one more lie, and pretend you'll miss me. God, I fucking miss you.

Love you always, Loyal

. . .

THE NOTE DROPPED TO LOYAL'S LAP. Loyal stared at nothing. Too many thoughts crowded his brain at once. His tongue wouldn't work.

"Are you okay, baby?"

At Toby's question, Loyal blinked. Toby came into focus. His expression was pinched—like he expected Loyal would fall apart now. "Is this the only reason you've been coming around, being nice to me?"

Toby drew back as if Loyal had slapped him. "No. Of course not." No one could look at him and call him a liar.

Loyal didn't feel better. "You didn't say anything. I guess I hoped this never made it to you."

As if his knees gave out, Toby dropped into the chair beside him. "You remember."

A sad smile pulled at Loyal's lips. He folded the note and tucked it beneath his thigh. "I never forgot."

"But your dad said you couldn't answer any questions about the wreck or anything that happened for at least three days beforehand."

Loyal forced himself to meet Toby's stare. "I wasn't supposed to live. Should I have told him that?"

Toby crossed his arms and chewed his thumbnail while staring at Loyal. Loyal had never felt more exposed. He couldn't breathe. His appetite was gone. Everything was over again. Loyal could practically feel his life crumbling apart.

He couldn't take it. "Say something."

Toby dropped his hand. "I'm so goddamn mad at you right now. Honestly, I don't know where to start."

It was every bit as bad as he thought. His gut wasn't lying to him. Loyal cleared his throat. His gaze skirted away. He couldn't look at Toby anymore. That flight to Tokyo, where Loyal had choked on his tears all the way to a new country, came back to haunt him again. That empty feeling, the one that screamed he had nothing left, was back. "It's okay." Loyal wouldn't make Toby do this anymore. He wouldn't keep stealing life from him. "I'll call... someone to come get me." He didn't know who. His dad was on shift for the next twenty-four hours with the fire station. Loyal's mind raced. A panic attack hit out of nowhere. He didn't know who to call. Loyal didn't have anyone anymore. Could he call a cab? He didn't know. Fuck. He didn't have any money. Loyal's eyes burned. Everything went blurry. He was drowning. Everything went dark at the edges of his vision. Maybe his heart had finally gone out after all the abuse. Did people suffocate when their heart stopped?

Toby's lips touched his and didn't move away. Loyal sucked a breath in through his nose. His lungs burned. The thoughts racing through his mind slowed. Toby lightly sucked his bottom lip, Loyal took another breath. He was with Toby. His heart didn't live inside his body. It hadn't stopped. Toby leaned back but he didn't release Loyal's face. Loyal hadn't even known he was holding it until that moment.

Toby swiped at Loyal's cheeks, wiping away tears Loyal hadn't known were falling. "Don't cry, baby. I don't want you to leave. It's just that you completely fucking terrified me with that confession. There's so much happening inside your head that you won't share. It scares me to my soul to think what you might do next. If you had succeeded, if you had —" Toby cleared his throat—like he choked on the words. "I would have lost the only reason I still get up every day. Do you have any idea how I drove myself insane, wondering what I had done to make you think you couldn't come to me? Why would you believe there is anything you could do that would make me slam the door in your face if you came here for help? Even if you had married Cameron and had a house full of kids, you could have come to me. I love you, Loyal." Toby dropped to his haunches at Loyal's feet and held his hands. He looked every bit as desperate as Loyal felt. "I'm your person," Toby said barely breaking a whisper. "Don't do that shit to me again, okay?"

Loyal couldn't look away. It broke his heart to think he was still hurting Toby. "I'm not going anywhere. When I woke up in the hospital, and I was alive and you were there, I felt like I'd been given a second chance. A chance to redeem myself. Another shot at doing right by you. You're my person too. I know you fell in love with someone with a lot of issues, but I'm trying, baby. You don't have to be scared. I'll find a way to be better for you."

Toby shook his head. "I don't want you to be better for me. You need to be better for you. I'll love you no matter what." Toby cast a quick glance around the kitchen before meeting Loyal's stare again. "Let's go take a shower, and then I'll take you out to breakfast instead."

Loyal hated that Toby was giving up on making breakfast together when he had been so excited about it earlier. "I thought you wanted to make breakfast together—like a real couple."

Heat flashed in Toby's eyes. "Right now, I think I'd rather fuck you in the shower—like a real couple."

"I love you." Loyal meant the words from the bottom of his soul. He knew Toby was mad at him for what he had done, but Loyal would make it better. He would fight—like no one had ever fought for Toby in his life. They were a real couple. No more secrets, even if it cost him everything, and it might. After all, no one outside this house knew Loyal was gay. Yeah. He still had to face that.

FIVE

AS HARD AS TOBY TRIED, he couldn't find anything to hold his attention with Loyal gone. He paced, printed out more directions for Mister, and checked Loyal's therapy schedule against his doctor's appointments. Nothing collided or needed to be moved. Toby paced some more. While he knew Orion and Loyal wouldn't be gone forever, this was the first time Loyal had been out of his sight since they—officially—became a couple. Toby was still a little gun shy over Loyal leaving the country. He knew it was dumb. Loyal wouldn't hop a plane today. Still. He wanted Loyal home.

Toby froze mid-step with the side of his fingernail in his mouth. That was the gist of things.

This was Loyal's home. He belonged under this roof. Toby needed Loyal to admit that.

"Holy shit, I forgot how horrible it is to be in the people-y public," Orion said, hauling two huge bags into the kitchen.

Loyal wheeled in behind him with two more perched on his lap. "It's definitely holiday shopping season. I rolled over two different people's toes. Hey, sexy," Loyal said, beaming up at Toby. His cheeks were flushed, and he looked happy. It was a beautiful sight.

Toby didn't hesitate to cross the room and steal a kiss before transferring his bags to the kitchen table where Orion had dumped the rest.

"Don't look in those bags," Orion fussed. "You have presents in there too."

Loyal swatted Toby's ass when he pretended to peek. "Don't tease him. Orion worked hard picking out the perfect gifts for y'all."

With a chuckle, Toby backed away from the table. He knew this was important to Orion. Orion had never celebrated Christmas. He had never had a Christmas tree with presents underneath. This would be his first with a real family. Toby wouldn't ruin that.

Loyal maneuvered into his usual spot at the

table. "I'm going to help him wrap these, so—at some point—you'll have to leave so we can wrap yours."

Toby blew out a rude noise. "Fine. But for now, I'm staying," he said, sounding childish even to his ears. "I want to see what everyone else got so I can lord it over them that I know."

"Seems fair," Orion said, sounding as serious as ever. His odd gray eyes locked on to Toby. "Thank you for letting me borrow Loyal today. He was a huge help. You know I hate going places. He even tolerated the bookstore like a champ."

Loyal shrugged. "I like books."

The doorbell rang. Orion pushed to his feet. "I'll grab that."

The moment he left the room, Toby jumped on his chance. "Quick. Show me my gift before he gets back."

"Stop," Loyal begged, laughing.

Orion returned with Jericho in tow before Toby could tease him more. Still, his smile wouldn't abate. "Jericho. Hey, man," Toby said, crossing the room and greeting Loyal's dad. "Are you coming to steal Loyal away? If so, Orion might fight you for him. He's already claimed him as free labor for the day."

"His labor isn't free." Orion sounded absent as he reclaimed his seat at the table. "He's getting paid in friendship currency. I'll repay the favor one day." Even though Orion sounded as serious as ever, "friendship currency" sounded suspiciously like something Tucker would say. Toby had a bad feeling his brother was rubbing off on his new husband.

Loyal laughed. It sounded evil. "I fully intend to make Orion drive me around town next week when I get my next insurance payment, so I can buy Christmas presents for everyone. Don't worry over me."

"I would love to do that," Orion said, sounding genuine. Tucker had won the lottery with Orion, and so had Toby, if he was being honest.

Jericho slapped Toby across the back. "Nah. I'm not here to steal Loyal. He does have physical therapy on Monday morning, though. So, please don't forget about that."

Toby nodded. "I have alerts set on my phone for all of his appointments. He won't miss any."

To Toby's surprise, Jericho shifted nervously. He looked uncomfortable. "Actually, I came by to talk to you, Toby. See, I was talking to Mister last night, and he was telling me a little more about your business. I was thinking, those clients of yours might be sick of you young pups. Maybe they're ready for a real man." He spread his arms wide, leaving no doubt who he meant.

Loyal sucked in a hiss. "My ears. I'll never be the same. Scarred for life by my own father."

A smile stretched Toby's lips at Loyal's antics, but he stayed focused on Jericho. Jericho was a good-looking guy. His job kept him in shape, and he looked like an older version of Loyal. That made him extra gorgeous in Toby's opinion. "I wouldn't be surprised if there were tons of potential customers looking for someone with more experience. If you're serious about this," Toby opened the back door inside the kitchen that led to the pool, "step into my office and we'll discuss it." With a soft chuckle, Jericho stepped through the door. Toby caught Loyal's eye. "I'll be back in a minute. Don't let Orion steal you away again before I get back."

Loyal winked and went back to helping Orion.

Reassured he would be fine, Toby followed Jericho outside and closed the door behind him. "I didn't know you dated," Toby said with a laugh as he moved to sit on the bottom step of the back porch, at the edge of the patio.

Jericho joined him. Side by side, they took up an uncomfortable amount of space. "I don't. Not anymore. Loyal has been my sole focus since... he was born, I guess. Everything else…" He shrugged, trailing off. "He's my kid," Jericho tacked on, as if that explained everything, and Toby supposed it did.

But Toby couldn't let it go at that. "You do realize I serve a very specific clientele, right? Have you ever dated a man?" Toby asked, getting straight to the point.

Jericho chuckled. "Nope, but I haven't dated a woman either in more years than I can count, so whatever. I'm not opposed to giving it a shot."

A snort escaped Toby. Jericho was wholly unique. "If you really want to try, I have no problem with that. I'm super curious as to why, though."

Jericho looked uncomfortable. "I don't want to impose upon your friendship with Loyal. This just sounds like something I could do in my spare time, and Loyal's hospital bills are really piling up past the point of bankrupting us. So, you know, if you think people might be interested in dating men their own age…"

"Loyal and I are more than friends," Toby said glossing over the hospital bills for now and refusing to hide behind that title. "No matter how Loyal tries to hide me," Toby tacked on, because Toby understood now that was the problem. Loyal was miserable to the point he was choking on it, because he couldn't say the words. Well, Toby had all the words, and he didn't mind saying them. He wouldn't let Loyal die from this. Toby wouldn't let fear kill the man he loved.

For a long minute, Jericho didn't say anything. He took a deep breath. His wide shoulders expanded. Then, to Toby's surprise, Jericho swiped at his eyes and cleared his throat. "I know. I've always known you two were more than friends. In fact, I probably knew before Loyal did. It's my fault he's like this. I should have... ugh." Jericho sounded every bit as frustrated as Toby had been feeling for months. "His mom, Amelia, has Loyal ever told you about her?"

Toby shook his head. "Not really. Just in passing. He said something once about how she was gone, but that's it."

Jericho snorted. "Oh, she's gone. She lives in Alabama with the husband and kids that won't doom her soul. Cunt."

Toby's eyebrows hit his hairline. Not only had Toby never heard Jericho talk bad about anyone, there was some real rage behind that name calling.

Jericho ripped some grass from the ground and tossed it aside. He didn't look Toby's way. "When Loyal was seven, she found a picture he had drawn of himself, holding another little boy's hand. She asked him about it, and Loyal confessed it was his boyfriend at school. He said they'd kissed on the tire swing."

Toby smiled at the thought. That was sweet.

Jericho visibly swallowed. His voice sounded strained. "By the time I got home from work, he was bleeding from countless lashes with a switch and was crying uncontrollably in the closet where he had been locked for hours. She told him that he would go to Hell and burn for eternity if he wouldn't let her fix him. I was enraged—like I wanted her dead. I called the police, took pictures of everything, and got full custody. After a year of supervised visits, she chose to sign away her rights."

Toby felt sick. He didn't know what to say. If anyone understood having a parent hurt them, it was Toby, but it murdered him to know anyone hurt Loyal. Jericho finally looked Toby's way. His eyes were bloodshot. "He just kind of shut down. I took him to a therapist. It seemed to help, but I should've seen that he didn't walk away from that unscarred. It was horrible, Toby. He didn't see a miserable piece of shit turning their back on their child. Loyal saw a devoted mother walking away from him because he was bad. I didn't know how to fix it. All I knew to do was be as supportive of him as I could possibly be. But I was so busy trying to be supportive, I didn't see that he was hiding himself in shame. I told myself he was a late bloomer when he didn't date anyone until high school. Then, when he started dating a girl, I thought the boy thing was just a phase. When you started coming around," Jericho shrugged. "I could see there was more between you two, but it wasn't my business." For a full minute Jericho didn't say anything. When he spoke again, he sounded like his words were for himself. "I should've made it my business." He tossed another handful of grass. "Maybe then, my son wouldn't have driven off a cliff and lost his shot at a normal life."

Toby blinked. There was a voice in the back of his head, screaming for him to keep his mouth shut. He couldn't. It was physically impossible. "He hasn't lost his shot at a normal life, but I wasn't aware you knew it was on purpose."

Jericho made a sound somewhere between a scoff and a grunt. "I didn't know. Not for sure. At least, not until now," he said, flashing Toby a gotcha grin, before blowing out a sigh. "I've been first on the scene for countless wrecks in the past twenty-five years. I've gotten pretty good at figuring out how they happened. Loyal's accident could've been an accident. It was entirely possible that—for whatever reason—he panicked and hit the gas instead of the brake before going over the edge at the lookout point. I told myself he might've been parked there and accidentally put the car in drive instead of reverse when he went to leave, but my gut knew. He always wore his seat belt, but he wasn't that night. Funnily enough, that's what saved him. He was thrown through the windshield before the car hit the ground." Jericho made a helpless gesture. "Then, he woke up. He didn't remember anything, and I was relieved. I just wanted him back. I didn't want to think about the weeks leading up to that wreck. It was easy to shrug off the way his smile had felt so faked that being around him was physically draining. The faker he got, the more I pretended to smile, hoping to make his happiness real. It's damn hard to help someone when they won't acknowledge anything is wrong. I just..." Jericho's hands rose and fell—like he had nothing.

Toby patted his shoulder. "It's not on you. Some people just can't reach for help. They just... can't. It's like it's worse if anyone knows."

For a long moment, Jericho stared at nothing. Finally, he turned his head and met Toby's gaze. "I don't know how to stop this from happening again.

He's so good at hiding himself. I don't know how to make him stop pretending so he can be happy without the fear of losing another parent. I'm not going anywhere, no matter what. But I don't know how to make him see it."

A smile pulled at the corners of Toby's mouth. It felt evil, even to him. "I know. Come on." He stood and waved for Jericho to follow. Together, they headed inside. Toby found Loyal where he left him—at the kitchen table. He had his bottom lip held between his teeth as he concentrated on taping one end of a present. Toby didn't slow or hesitate as he moved to stand behind Loyal's chair. His hand slid across Loyal's throat, before moving upward. He gently but firmly tilted Loyal's chin up, where he couldn't get away. All he could do was focus on Toby. "You look like you're having fun."

Loyal smiled. Real happiness shone bright in his eyes. "I am. Orion bought—"

Toby bent and captured Loyal's mouth, cutting off his words. He didn't hesitate or take mercy on him. There could be no mistaking the kiss for anything other than it was—real love. A claiming. Toby poured his heart into it, ensuring there could be no doubt that Loyal felt his love and everyone could see it. He left Loyal no choice but to do the same, because he knew Loyal felt the same.

With one final suck of Loyal's bottom lip, he lightly kissed Loyal's chin, and then leaned away. "So, with your dad accepting dates now, he'll probably be gone a lot at night. I was just telling him outside, I think you should move in here with me."

A flash of panic crossed Loyal's features, as reality obviously sank in. He had kissed Toby with his dad feet away. A small part of Toby wanted to pat his own back. After all, he had managed to make Loyal forget where he was, but a bigger part of Toby hoped Loyal didn't let him down.

Loyal's gaze moved Jericho's way. At some point, Jericho had claimed a chair at the table, and was now staring back at Loyal, looking like nothing out of the ordinary happened. Toby was proud of him. He was a good dad. Loyal didn't know how lucky he was. Loyal swiped his palms on his thighs. "Um, so you got the job, huh?"

Jericho chuckled. "Did you doubt me? I told you I've still got it. Toby seems to think men might date me."

Loyal's eyebrows couldn't have gotten any closer to his hairline if he tried. He cleared his throat. It was an uncomfortable sound. "You'll be dating men?"

Jericho shrugged. "Well, I mean, that's his clientele. I wouldn't have approached Toby about this if I wasn't willing."

For a moment, Loyal visibly floundered, as if he didn't know where to go with that. Then, he went completely still, as if something clicked in his mind. "Wait." He turned in his chair and stared up at Toby. "Did you just ask me to move in with you?"

Toby smiled. He poured as much wickedness as he could muster into the gesture. "You're mine. I want you here."

"He's a Kodiak," Orion said, setting aside one gift and starting on another. "You may as well say yes. Trust me on this one. He'll have his way no matter what." Orion paused and met Loyal's gaze. "In fact, you may as well start telling people you're married now. It's already too late for you."

Toby's smile grew to the point his cheeks ached. Orion sounded so serious while Loyal looked like a fast-moving train had hit him. Jericho was reading the backs of the books Orion bought—like this was every day for him. Toby could barely contain his happiness. Loyal would give him everything. He felt it in his gut.

LOYAL SAT IN A HAZE AS HE TRIED TO DECIDE what happened to his life while wrapping gift after gift on autopilot. One second, he had been trying to figure out how to gracefully slip from the closet with his dad. The next, his dad was making plans to start dating men and Toby was kissing Loyal in a display of ownership three feet from his father. Obviously, the matter was settled, but Loyal felt... weird. Like the other shoe would drop any second and Loyal would be homeless, broken-hearted, and without a family. It seemed odd for things to be so anti-climactic. He had spent years near hyperventilation just thinking about anyone realizing he was a fake. Years of therapy told him that was all on his mom abandoning him, but still. Everyone acted like this was no big deal and Loyal still expected to get beaten and locked away. He didn't know how to cope.

"You know what we should do," Jericho said, cutting into Loyal's silent panic attack. "We should all go to Howling Twister tonight. Loyal hasn't been up there since the accident and they helped us a lot when they raised money for Loyal's hospital bills. You should go and let them see how good you're doing."

Loyal cast a look around the table, gauging interest in Jericho's suggestion. In truth, he kind of liked the idea. He didn't get to go out much, since it was hard work. Being out with Orion today made him realize how much he missed the active lifestyle he had before his life went to shit. Plus, his dad looked hopeful. "Yeah. If everyone else is in, I am too."

Toby massaged his shoulders. "Sounds good to me. I could handle some loud music and beer."

Orion looked a bit panicked. "No thanks. Unless Tucker wants to go when he gets home, that is. I'm not much on bars."

Loyal understood. Orion was the quiet type. He liked silence. "Don't worry over it. You should take advantage of having an empty house when Tucker gets home. You're a newlywed after all."

Orion flashed him a grateful smile for the save. "That sounds like a good plan."

Jericho rapped his knuckles on the table. "It's settled then. Should we meet there at seven?"

Toby kissed the side of Loyal's neck. "Sounds good. That gives us plenty of time to eat and all that."

"Agreed. I'll see y'all at seven," Jericho said, coming to his feet.

The moment he was gone, Toby pounced. "Hey, Orion. If you don't mind, I need to steal Loyal."

Orion nodded as he cut a square of wrapping paper. "That's fine. I'm almost done, so no worries." He met Loyal's stare. "Thank you so much for going with me today. When I get back from Aspen, let me know when you want me to take you shopping. We'll grab lunch or something too while we're out."

The smile tugging at the corners of Loyal's mouth was out of his control. Orion felt like a real friend and Loyal needed that more than anyone could possibly know. "I'd love that."

Toby bent and kissed Loyal beneath his ear as he took control of Loyal's wheelchair. "Let's go, sexy."

Loyal had to take a breath. He never got tired of Toby's lips on his skin. Toby pushed him down the hall and into his bedroom. He closed the door behind them. Loyal's anxiety kicked up. Toby was being too quiet and looking serious. It didn't take much to raise Loyal's blood pressure nowadays. He was pretty much always a complete wreck.

Toby's bedroom was huge with one half as a normal bedroom—king bed, dresser, chest, and nightstands. The bathroom door marked the center of the room and the other half was like a small sitting room—love seat, TV, and bookcase. Toby steered

Loyal to the love seat and sat down facing him. His too serious expression had Loyal's heartbeat pounding in his ears.

Toby took his hands. "Baby, if you don't want to live with me, it's okay to say so. I'll still love you and want to be with you no matter what."

Confusion had Loyal's forehead furrowing. "What are you talking about?"

"I asked you to move in. You quickly changed the subject and jumped on the chance to make plans for the night—like you were hoping I would forget I asked."

Loyal blinked. Honestly, he had been sideswiped by so much in such a short time he was the one who had forgotten. "Is that really what you want? I mean, right now, I'm a lot of work and that might not change. At least four days a week, I have some sort of appointment. Not to mention, all the remodeling you just did at my dad's house. I know you've done a bit here too, but nothing like you've done there. Plus, your place is huge. I know you don't want the extra expense of trying to make this place easy to navigate for me, because, baby, this might be the best I'll ever be. I might not ever get out of this chair."

Toby listened patiently until Loyal made his way

down the list of ways he was inconveniencing Toby's life. "Are you finished?"

Loyal held his breath to stop himself from saying more and nodded.

A sweet smile hovered on Toby's lips—like he knew Loyal fought the urge to keep going. "I can't think of anything I'd rather spend my dad's money on than the person I love the most. Remodeling this entire place is nothing when compared to how far I would go for you. As to your appointments, I have way more time to take you than your dad does. Plus, you don't need to be thinking about how you'll pay for things. You have me. I promise you don't need anything else. I'll always take care of you." Toby made it sound so simple—like Loyal could just land here and he would be fine. No guilt. When Loyal didn't respond, Toby's eyebrows rose. "Are you still thinking it over, or are you trying to find a way to say no?"

Loyal shook his head. "Actually, I was thinking I've never done a damn thing in my life to deserve you." Loyal's eyes stung as he made the confession.

"Life doesn't have a damn thing to do with deserve. I'm not sure why people think that," Toby added the last bit as if more for himself.

The burning behind Loyal's eyes doubled. "I

just fucking love you. You know that, right? Like I was a fucked-up mess before you. Maybe I still am a little bit of a mess, but you saved me. You always do, and I'd be failing you if I didn't stop for a second and say that you deserve someone better than me."

"There you go with that deserve again. The fact is, I don't *want* anyone but you."

"I don't want anyone but you either," Loyal said, confessing the only truth that mattered. "Since you pretty much just threw me out of the closet with my dad earlier, there's no reason for me to say no."

A hint of a smile touched Toby's lips. "I didn't realize you were hiding us." Funny how Toby's words sounded like the lie they were, but Loyal let it go.

"Promise me you'll tell me if I'm too much and you need a break."

"It'll never happen," Toby said scooting closer and running his hands up Loyal's thighs. The heat in his eyes had Loyal's mouth going dry. "So, we have around two hours until we need to be at the bar. I could take you to dinner first." The way he touched Loyal said they wouldn't be having dinner.

"Or we could stop somewhere afterward."

Toby looked comically taken aback by Loyal's

suggestion. "But then what will we do for the next two hours."

Loyal's entire body relaxed even as it burned. "I'm sure you can find a way to entertain me."

In one swift motion, Toby swept Loyal from his chair and into his lap. "You're right. I have tricks galore to keep you busy." Toby claimed his mouth. While turned sideways, sprawled across Toby's lap, all Loyal could do was hold Toby's neck and accept his fate. Toby was in charge. As their tongues clashed, Toby tugged at Loyal's clothes. A moan escaped Loyal as he found his dick in Toby's capable hand. With one arm wrapped around him, Toby held him in place while he massaged Loyal's cock. Loyal bit and sucked at Toby's lips while Toby took no mercy on him.

Loyal had no idea how he ended up with his pants and underwear down past his knees, but Toby was like a magician. He stroked, rolled, probed, and thrust, making Loyal's mind a mess. Even with the loss of some sensation to the lower half of his body, Toby was mind blowing. Loyal did what he could to make Toby every bit as insane. He massaged Toby's erection through his jeans. His over-the-pants hand job was at an awkward angle, but the way Toby's breathing turned ragged said angles didn't mean shit.

Toby picked up the pace, jacking Loyal's cock faster and stealing Loyal's thoughts. Loyal became nothing but a ball of need and want. He ripped his mouth away, threw his head back and sucked air.

"That's it, sexy," Toby growled, sounding hot as hell. "Fuck my hand, baby. I want to watch while you come unglued. You're so goddamn gorgeous. I want you to ruin my clothes the way you've already ruined me for anyone else. Shoot that cum all over me. I want it."

Between Toby's words and the pressure beating at his crown, Loyal didn't stand a chance. A cry tore from his throat as cum shot from his dick.

Toby whimpered like the orgasm was his. "Fuck. That's sexy." With cum still coating his hand, Toby clasped Loyal's jaw and forced Loyal to meet his stare. He looked intense. On fire. "I'm about to fuck you, because I love you and you need to know you belong to me."

Goddamn. It was true. Toby had owned Loyal since the first minute they met. Nothing would ever change that. It was well past the time he should accept his fate. He was home.

SIX

TRUTHFULLY, Toby was a bit tired. After spending the day trying to find something to keep him busy, making love to Loyal, and now coming out on the town, he needed a nap. Maybe he was getting old. Settled. A smiled curved his lips. He was good with being settled.

Howling Twister looked like a huge cabin on the outside and a honkytonk on the inside. Neon lights covered the walls, advertising every beer under the sun. Country music blared from the speakers, periodically interrupted by a DJ. People in cowboy hats line danced in perfect time. Truthfully, it wasn't Toby's type of place, but the owners were big on supporting the military and local emergency services. Since Loyal's dad was a fireman, they treated him like a rock star and hadn't hesitated to donate an entire night of profits toward Loyal's hospital bills. The least they could do was show up and let the people see Loyal's face.

Toby bent and touched his lips to Loyal's ear in between people trying to talk to him. "Would you like a beer?"

Loyal shook his head. "Last time I had alcohol, the next morning was horrible. I think I'll stick to water."

Without thought and under the guise of talking to Loyal, Toby kissed the shell of Loyal's ear. "If you want one beer, I'll make sure your morning is better than last time."

Laughing eyes flashed his way. "Why did that sound so sexual falling from your lips?"

Toby's smirk was out of his control. "Because you know me. Now, would you like a beer?"

"Hey, Loyal. Hey, Toby."

Loyal's head whipped around at the interruption. Toby didn't immediately look Cameron's way. It took him a moment to look away from Loyal's reaction. He looked horrified. A tiny crack formed in Toby's heart. He had a terrible feeling in his gut as he straightened away from Loyal and focused on Cameron.

"Hey, Cam. It's been a while." Toby didn't think he did that great of job hiding his animosity, even though she hadn't done anything wrong.

She flashed Toby a smile and focused on Loyal. She looked nervous. Her fingers went to the ends of her short hair, as if worrying if she looked okay.

Loyal sounded twice as unhappy to see her. "I thought you were still in Tokyo."

Her smile faltered a bit at Loyal's tone. "Things didn't really pan out there. I got back last week, and I just heard about your accident." She motioned uncomfortably toward his chair. "That's why I haven't been by your dad's place to check on you."

"I don't live with my dad."

Cameron shifted from one foot to the other and clasped her hands in front of her. "Oh. So, how have you been otherwise?"

Toby felt a little bad for her. She was trying and Loyal wasn't making things easier. Toby didn't know whether to cheer or cry. He had always liked Cameron despite kind of hating her because she had the only thing Toby couldn't live without. The thing was, Cameron was nice. She was hard to hate.

Jericho appeared out of nowhere and handed Loyal a beer. "Hey, Cammie girl. When did you get back in town?"

Cameron's smile brightened. "Last week. Sorry I haven't been by."

"It's all right. I'm rarely home these days."

It hadn't escaped Toby's notice that Loyal wasn't saying a word. Toby squeezed his shoulder, hoping to break whatever terrible rhetoric had taken over his mind.

"Would you like to dance?" Jericho asked when Loyal still didn't say anything.

Even though Cameron looked taken aback, she nodded. "Sure." She took Jericho's arm when he moved to her side, but she still looked over her shoulder at Loyal with longing in her eyes. "It was good seeing you."

Loyal didn't return her words.

Toby broke. Something was up. He dropped to his haunches beside Loyal's chair. "Are you okay, baby?"

Loyal held the beer out. "Do you want this?"

Toby shook his head. "I'm driving. Do you plan to talk to me or leave me guessing?"

With a shrug, Loyal seemed to get smaller. There was a hint of desperation in his eyes. "I just had like a thousand realizations hit me at once. She walked up and all I could think was that I owe you like a million apologies. Cameron was talking and all I could think about was all the times you took a backseat to her and I'm so goddamn mad at myself. If I just would have..." Loyal looked defeated. "Nobody cared I'm gay but me."

Toby loved him. "To be fair, Cameron probably would have."

A snort of laughter escaped Loyal. His mood lightened. Loyal glanced around, as if taking in their surroundings before meeting Toby's stare again. "Do you want to get out of here?"

He didn't have to ask Toby twice. Toby plucked the beer from Loyal's hand, set it on the closest table, and took control of his chair so they could get through the crowd as fast as possible. With Loyal's handicap tag, they didn't have to go far to get to Toby's truck. Since they had plenty of practice, he got Loyal in the passenger seat in no time. As he helped Loyal with his seat belt, Loyal struck. He snagged Toby's collar and pulled him closer. His mouth covered Toby's. Their surroundings disappeared. His heart beat faster. Happiness overflowed inside him. Every time Loyal made the first move, Toby was blown away anew. This was his life and he could barely believe it. The man he had dreamed about forever was his. He had agreed to move in with Toby. Loyal wasn't hiding him from anyone. This was everything he had ever hoped they could be. Toby had never had so much to lose.

"I love you," Loyal whispered as he changed angles. For a moment, Loyal sucked his bottom lip. He cupped Toby's face and moved away, holding his stare. Loyal looked turned on and in love. That last bit left Toby speechless. "You're my best friend." Loyal's words punched Toby in the chest and he didn't know why. Maybe because, even though he knew that, hearing the words aloud gave them power. "I have literally nothing to offer you, but I love you more than anyone ever could. That I will give you every day. I'm sorry I wasn't brave when you needed me to be. It'll never happen again. You should get in the truck. I'm about to suck your dick."

"Goddamn." The breathless curse escaped Toby with no input from his brain. Loyal was so fucking hot. Toby couldn't stop himself from stealing one more kiss.

"Oh. That makes sense."

Toby's head jerked back at the words. Cameron stood two feet away, looking at everything but directly at them. She twisted the hem of her t-shirt. Toby quickly readjusted his flannel, ensuring his erection was hidden. "Cam, hey. I didn't see you there." Yeah. Toby knew he sounded like an idiot. It was out of his control.

Cameron's gaze slid back their way. Her spine visibly straightened. "I wanted to apologize before you disappeared," she said, focusing on Loyal. "I did and said a lot of shitty things while we were in Tokyo. You were all I had there, and I was frustrated with the situation, but I see now it wasn't all me." She looked between them again. "Or maybe it was," she tacked on, sounding absent. "I think I knew I was standing between you two and I just refused to budge." She looked determined as her gaze locked onto Loyal. "I hope you've finally found the happiness that's eluded you your whole life."

"I have." Toby's gaze jumped to Loyal at the firmly spoken words. He looked exactly like a man making a vow. No one could look at him and doubt the truth. He belonged to Toby. "I'm sorry things went so badly there at the end, but I can't apologize for how things turned out. Toby deserves better. I was hiding from myself, and... he's just entitled to more from me now."

Cameron's gaze slid between them once more. She gave them a sharp nod. "I wish you two the best, then. It's overdue, I think." Without another word, Cameron walked away.

Toby focused on Loyal. He was staring at Toby.

Loyal brushed his fingers through Toby's hair, making his eyes fall closed. "I love you, Toby Kodiak."

A smile that came from his heart spread across Toby's lips. "I love you too."

"I would very much like to go home now and do that sloppy head thing I promised."

Toby snorted, but he couldn't stop smiling. He was so in love with this man. Possibly they took a thousand backroads to end up where they belonged, but they were still here. Toby would never stop fighting. What they had was everything.

THE WAY TOBY TRAILED HIS FINGERS UP AND down the back of Loyal's arm had Loyal's eyes growing heavy. He refused to go to sleep. The sound of Toby's heartbeat against Loyal's ear held him fascinated. He never dreamed he could love someone so much that the sound of their heartbeat would be everything to him. It had been a full day, for sure. Still, Loyal wasn't ready for it to end. In truth, Loyal was a little scared to fall asleep. He wasn't the sanest of people. It was entirely possible he would wake up tomorrow and learn this was a hallucination. Loyal wasn't mentally prepared for that. Unconsciously, his hold tightened on Toby. He needed something good.

"Are you okay?"

Loyal nodded against Toby's chest at the question. "I'm just savoring the moment."

A sexy chuckle caressed his ears. "Same. Logically, I know you'll be right here from now on, but I'm still scared to go to sleep and miss a second."

They were so much alike. Hot messes. Loyal remembered something he had forgotten in the midst of a crazy day. "Hey, with Orion and Tucker leaving for Aspen, do you need some help with the business —like filling in for Orion or whatever. I don't know what he does exactly, but I can help with whatever." Loyal bit his lip. He didn't want to push his way too far into Toby's life. Sometimes, he didn't know where the line was. Toby didn't answer right away, and Loyal wasn't brave enough to wait. "Never mind. It was just a thought. You don't have to think up a way to not hurt my feelings. Like I said, I don't even know what Orion does."

Toby squeezed him until he stopped rambling. "It's not that. I would love your help. Your question just reminded me I need to talk to you about the business. Um." Toby sounded uncomfortable. "So, I'm kind of booked for this next weekend." He hesitated, making Loyal worry he wouldn't like where this went. "Like with a date."

"Oh, well, I know what you do so that's no surprise."

Toby squeezed him again, making Loyal chuckle over Toby's obvious annoyance. "The thing is, if your dad is serious about joining the team, then I have enough people that I can back away from taking dates." Loyal started to say he didn't have to do that, but Toby kept talking. "But I'd like to keep my appointment on Saturday night first. That guy, Kevin, is one of our first clients and he confessed some stuff to me last time we went out. I'm afraid, if I cancel our appointment, he'll think he did something wrong."

"I love you." Loyal couldn't stop the words. Toby was good. Loyal didn't know if Toby saw it, but he was an awesome human. He always worried more about other people than he did himself. Sometimes, Loyal wondered if Toby's father would still be alive if not for Tanner and Tucker's existence. That had been his breaking point. One day, he had woken up incapable of seeing them harmed any longer. He had sent them away with money he had pickpocketed at a nearby restaurant. Once they were gone, he had ensured they would never get hurt again. He hadn't walked away from that unscarred, mentally or physically. But Loyal knew, Toby survived because he had stayed true to his role—the caretaker. Now, it was Loyal's job to take care of Toby and he would. "You do whatever you feel is right, baby. I know you. More than that, I trust you. You're not a cheat. I know, if you accept a client, it's for a good reason and that reason can't touch us. You always do what's right. I don't doubt for a second this is any different."

For a long moment, Toby didn't respond, but his fingertips never stopped trailing up and down Loyal's arm. Loyal knew he was lost in thought. He was fine to wait. "Did I do the right thing starting this business?"

Toby's question surprised Loyal. Of all the thoughts he had expected might be going through Toby's head, that wasn't one of them. "What makes you ask that?"

He felt Toby shrug. "I had good intentions, but I'm not sure if I'm really helping anyone. At first, I thought this would be a good way to help people get paid what they deserve by setting a standard on our site. Not to mention, we could help keep the guys safe. Honestly, though, I'm not sure I'm doing anything at all. I mean, Orion and Tucker are handling the management side of things—customer support, employee complaints, and security. Tanner is meeting new faces and signing people up to offer their services on our site. I'm just going on the occasional date and making a few calls. Maybe I should just hand this off to Tucker and Tanner. None of us need the money, but maybe it's unfair for me to be taking any of the cut from this."

Loyal moved up onto his elbow and punched Toby in the ribs. Not hard enough to hurt but enough to get his attention.

"What the fuck?" Toby asked, rubbing his side.

Loyal refused to feel bad. "That one was from Tucker. Do I need to call Tanner and ask if he would like me to pass along another from him? You know damn well the three of you are a team. Always. On everything. It's impossible for either of those guys to feel like you're dead weight just like you could never feel that way about them. If you feel useless, then keep accepting dates. If you don't want to accept dates, then take some of the workload off everyone else. You're right. People do need this. Do you think my dad would've felt comfortable enough to go to anyone else and offer to go on dates for pay? Hell no. And he needs the money, baby. He signed all the paperwork at the hospital, assuming financial responsibility while I was too far gone to intercede. Maybe one of these days, I'll be able to work again and help, but until then, all my fucking bills are going to him. He needs this. You gave him that outlet, and I don't doubt for a second there are dozens of men who feel the same about what you're doing."

Toby snagged Loyal's waist and hauled him across his body like a blanket until Loyal clung to his chest while staring down into his eyes. "Your dad doesn't have anything to worry about because I already planned to pay off your bills before he asked to join the site."

Loyal blinked. He didn't know how to respond. On one hand, Toby shouldn't be responsible for all Loyal's debt. On the other, neither should Loyal's dad. On both hands, what the fuck? "How am I supposed to respond to that? I already feel like shit because I buried my dad in debt. Now, I have twice the culpability here. At least Dad is my dad. He signed on to me forever by bringing me into the world. But you have no real reason to do this."

Toby's eyebrows rose. "I'm going to pretend you didn't just insult the ever-living fuck out of me with that one. Instead, I'll argue you are every bit my responsibility because you'll be my husband by Christmas."

Just when Loyal thought he couldn't be more stunned by anything Toby did or said, he pulled that one out of the bag. "I'm sorry, what?"

Toby nodded like it was settled. "I've waited literally years for you to come around. If you think I'm waiting even one more month to lock you down, and giving you a chance to slip away, you're fucking insane."

"I think we both know damn well I'm insane."

A sexy growl came from the back of Toby's throat, making it hard for Loyal to hold on to his irritation. "Are you really going to fight me on this?"

"Of course I'm not," Loyal said, matching Toby's hostile tone.

"Seriously—" Toby froze mid-speech as Loyal's words obviously sank in. "Wait. Did you just agree to marry me?"

"Of course I did. I'm not a complete idiot. You're not the only one who's been waiting literally years."

For a long moment, Toby stared at him in silence. "Holy shit," he breathed, sounding blown away. "I don't know who to call first, but I want to tell everyone."

Loyal dropped his forehead to Toby's chest and

laughed. Happiness owned him. He never knew it could be so empowering to have someone this proud to be with him.

"If I call either of my brothers, the other one will be mad they weren't first."

Loyal really didn't care who knew first. He just liked fucking with Toby. "If you tell your brothers first, my dad's feelings will be hurt."

"Shit. I didn't think of that."

"Maybe you could kiss me," Loyal suggested. "And then, if you're still set on telling everyone right now, then we could call everyone via conference call and tell everyone at once. But I feel moved to remind you, it's one in the morning."

"You're right." Toby rolled and crushed Loyal to the bed. "I should focus on you, instead. We can tell them tomorrow."

Loyal liked this plan. In fact, maybe he could convince Toby to stay in bed tomorrow too. Their families would still be waiting when they came up for air. For now, they needed some time to savor their new life.

SEVEN

TOBY EXPECTED his date with Kevin to be awkward. In truth, it was nice. Kevin talked about his job. Apparently, selling homes to millionaires was interesting work. He made Toby wonder what kind of customer he had been when searching for a house to share with his brothers. They had been somewhat picky, because they had wanted to stay together, but they also wanted their own space. Plus, they were accustomed to living outdoors. They had to find some ways to hang on to that. That's how they had ended up with the perfect pool that looked like a natural body of water, and on the edge of Lake Travis where they were free to go out on the water without fighting a crowd.

Kevin had a ton of crazy stories, keeping Toby

laughing through dinner. He seemed so at ease that Toby was too. Until they started back to Toby's house, that is. Then, it set in that he couldn't avoid talking to Kevin any longer. He had to tell him he wouldn't be accepting anymore dates with anyone. The last thing Toby wanted was for Kevin to think his decision had anything to do with that kiss. Toby took a breath. It was now or never.

Kevin pulled to the side of the road without warning. "This is the last time I'm hiring you," he said fast, like ripping off a bandage.

Toby blinked. He didn't know how to react since he had been trying to find a way all night to say the exact same thing.

"You didn't do anything wrong," Kevin rushed to add, as if he expected Toby to argue. "Since our last date, I've been really thinking about my life. I'm not ready. My heart can't take the beating. Even though I know there are lots of fish in the sea, there are a lot of duds too. In this day and age, everyone wants to keep things casual—leave their options open. I'm not a casual guy. That's why your business served my needs so well. I knew I could hire someone to spend time with me and there was zero pressure for it to be more. It's not meant to be anything but a fun date. I think—

maybe—I don't even have that in me yet. I'm sorry."

Kevin was always open and honest with Toby—real. Toby needed to be the same, because he didn't want Kevin to feel guilty. There was no need. Not only was Toby simply providing a service, his heart belonged to Loyal. "That's perfect, actually," Toby said, smiling. He rubbed Kevin's arm, connecting with him. "I was dreading dropping the news that I won't be accepting anymore dates from anyone after tonight. After our kiss, I did a lot of thinking too. There's only one person for me. He'll always be it. So, I threw myself on his mercy and he's giving me a real shot. I don't want to mess it up, even for my business."

The way Kevin smiled at the confession made Toby glad he had been open. Kevin didn't need the extra burden of thinking he disappointed Toby in any way. "That's awesome. That gives me hope there are still good people left in the world." Kevin held out his hand for a handshake. "I'm glad to have met you, Toby Kodiak. I hope you have an amazing life."

Toby shook his hand, holding on longer than necessary before letting him go. "You too, Kevin Abbot. If I ever see you out, please don't act like I'm a stranger."

"Deal," Kevin said, as he switched on his blinker, signaling his move back onto the road.

The air changed in the car. Lightened. The pressure that had been sitting on Toby's chest, each time he thought about dropping his news, eased. He was glad to be done with this part of Cubs for Rent. When his brothers and he first had this idea, they never expected to be doing any actual dating. Now that they were all in relationships, Toby couldn't see any of them with anyone else. They needed to take on their real roles now, looking out for the guys who listed their services through them. Everything would be okay, even if the business failed. Toby would be good. He had Loyal. Nothing else mattered.

As they reached Toby's house, Kevin maneuvered down the driveway, stopping behind a line of cars Toby hadn't expected to see tonight. He recognized Jericho's truck. He couldn't make out what was parked in front of that. Not to mention, the action taking place in front of the garage doors is what really held him captivated.

"Looks like there's a party going on."

Toby was every bit as surprised as Kevin sounded. While it wasn't uncommon for his brothers to dust off the grill on nice days, and it had been extra warm for December this year, this was extra, and Tucker wasn't around to take the blame. Not only did the smell of grilled food fill the air, several people were beneath the basketball goal, looking like they were invested in winning. One of those people was Loyal. In fact, he had the ball and was fiercely trying to shoot while Tanner tried to steal.

Kevin laughed. "It looks like they're having fun."

Toby nodded—dumbfounded. He had forgotten how competitive Loyal was. "Seems so."

Kevin ran his hand along the steering wheel. "So... which of these guys is yours?"

Toby motioned Loyal's way. "The one with the ball."

Kevin's mouth lifted in one corner. "That fits."

With raised eyebrows, Toby held Kevin's stare. "How so?"

"He's the prettiest," Kevin said, sounding oddly sad.

Keeping with their newfound roles, and Toby's request that Kevin not pretend they were strangers, he motioned toward the game. "Would you like to meet him?"

Kevin was back to looking uncomfortable. "Won't that be weird for him?"

"Not at all. Loyal is pretty amazing. Truthfully,

he might actually feel better about me going out tonight if he meets you."

While chewing his bottom lip, Kevin stared at Tanner, Henry, Jericho, and Loyal playing ball for a moment longer. Finally, he smiled. "All right."

They stepped from the car at the same time and met at the front. Side by side, they approached the game. Loyal shot, making the basket. Jericho raced to his side and high-fived him. "Hell, yeah, boy. Show them what's up."

"That was awesome."

At Kevin's observation, everyone turned their way. A bright smile lit Loyal's face. He wheeled closer. It was obvious he wanted to properly greet Toby, but he didn't know his place at the moment.

"I'm Kevin," Kevin said, holding his hand out for Loyal to shake. "Toby tells me you're his better half."

Loyal moved closer and accepted Kevin's handshake. "I don't know about better, but definitely his other half. I'm Loyal."

"Love that name."

"That's a compliment for me," Jericho said with a laugh. When Kevin looked his way, Jericho made a dismissive gesture. "I'm his dad. You can ignore me. I've been drinking."

Kevin's smile grew. He truly looked like he was

enjoying himself—like there was nothing out of the ordinary going on here. "There's no way you're old enough to be his dad. I call bullshit."

Jericho blushed, taking Toby by surprise. He didn't know Jericho was capable of blushing. "I'm a fire fighter. I have to stay in shape. Seriously, you can stop me any time and save me from myself."

Toby fought a laugh. Jericho was really embarrassed, which obviously turned to awkwardness for him, and Toby couldn't look away. Apparently, this spoke to Kevin on some level because he couldn't stop smiling or staring at Jericho. Loyal took advantage of the distraction and took Toby's hand. He kissed Toby's knuckles while no one was watching. Toby winked. He was ridiculously happy to be home with Loyal.

"We're cooking out. If you haven't eaten, you should join us," Jericho offered, bringing Toby's attention back to the group.

Before Kevin could respond, the back door opened, and Mister stepped out. Mister froze. His gaze locked on Kevin. Kevin's smile slipped away. Mister's gaze slid Toby's way. He looked between them, obviously putting together that Kevin was his date for the night. His expression hardened. Toby almost took a step back. Mister looked ready to commit murder.

"So, this is the client you kissed?" Mister asked as he stormed down the back steps.

Toby's gaze shot to Loyal. Mister could not fuck up his life. Toby couldn't survive that.

Loyal looked between them. His forehead furrowed.

Mister didn't stop there. "Are you being fucking serious, Toby? Kevin is the client who sent you those flowers. The one you kissed last weekend. Are you fucking joking?"

Kevin turned away, heading back toward his car without a word to anyone.

Mister kept talking like he wasn't ruining Toby's life. "Is it not enough that you already have one man so sickeningly in love with you that he drove off a cliff when he thought you wouldn't be together? Now you need to seduce my ex too? Fuck this," Mister growled, taking off toward the lake.

Toby's gaze moved from Mister's retreating back to Loyal. Shock kept him frozen in place. He still didn't understand what happened.

Loyal motioned Kevin's way. "You go after that one. I've got this one." Loyal spun his chair around and went after Mister.

Jericho pushed Toby Loyal's way. "I've got Kevin. You go after Loyal. Don't give Mister time to make matters worse."

In a stunned haze, Toby headed in the direction Loyal disappeared. He had thought his life was finally going to be all right. Toby had truly believed he would be good. Maybe this was his punishment. Maybe murderers didn't get to have a happy ending. Before Toby caught up with Loyal, he veered left and headed for the lake. Maybe Loyal was better off without him. It was possible life would always be this way with him. Loyal deserved someone better.

"ARE YOU REALLY RUNNING FROM A GUY IN A wheelchair?" Loyal was too fucking irritated to care if he was using his injuries to guilt Mister into stopping.

Mister spun on him, looking enraged. "Are you really playing that card?"

"Yes." Loyal didn't feel an ounce of shame, especially after what Mister had just pulled. "Do you feel better about yourself after that show?"

Mister ran both hands through his hair and paced away. "I'm sorry. I'm just... ugh." Mister growled loudly. Oddly, Loyal related more with that one sound than he had related with anything ever. Mister faced him again, looking wrecked. "Why do you look so calm? Don't you want to go back and kick Kevin's ass for touching Toby? Aren't you infuriated that Toby let me read the letter you sent him? Because I sure as hell want to go back and kill Toby."

Loyal shrugged. "Not really, no."

Mister's face screwed up with confusion. "Why the fuck not?"

A strange calm settled over Loyal in the face of Mister's jealous rage. "Because loving me hurts," Loyal said, choosing to be one hundred percent honest with Mister and himself. "If, for a moment, Kevin took away the misery Toby has suffered because he loves me, how should I feel?"

Mister tilted his chin up. He blinked rapidly at the sky as if fighting the emotions overwhelming him. "Yeah. I get that," he said after a minute. "Loving me hurts too. Turns out, being my friend isn't so great either. I shouldn't have said that shit. I already wish I could take back the last ten minutes." Mister looked completely wrecked. Loyal got it. "I'm just," Mister's hands lifted and fell, "a bad person, I think."

Loyal took a deep breath. He wasn't really in any place mentally to give advice, but neither could he say nothing after what Mister had just done. Loyal clasped his hands in his lap so they wouldn't shake and dove in. "Look, I don't know what happened between that guy and you. I saw his face, though. When you stepped outside, I saw the way he looked when he saw you. Only real love levels someone to that extent. Maybe he'll never forgive you for whatever you've done that gave him that look. I don't know. But maybe you need to go back and apologize so you can start working on forgiving yourself, because if I recognize anything, it's the debilitating guilt I see in you. You see where hating myself got me," Loyal said, spreading his arms wide and laying himself bare. "Hurting the person you love most in the world, is a slow bleed in your soul. I hope you find a way to cauterize that before you find a new way to ruin your life like I did. You can storm off now, if you want. I won't think less of you. But next time you see Toby, you will fucking apologize for the shit you just pulled or don't come back here." Loyal liked Mister and he understood his position, but Toby was his. No one hurt him.

With a sharp nod, Mister walked away. For a moment, Loyal stared at his retreating form. His heart hurt. Toby's face as Mister had slung his accusations wouldn't leave Loyal. Then, there was the fact that Mister knew about Loyal's suicide attempt and he had flung that out there for everyone to hear. Loyal didn't know how to feel. As he turned to head back to the house, Loyal caught sight of Toby sitting alone on the boat dock. Loyal swore he could feel the pain rolling off Toby from across the yard. Loyal followed the path Toby had built for him. He stopped a few feet away and stared at the back of the man he loved more than life. In fact, he had been fully prepared to throw his life away when he was sure he wouldn't get to spend it with Toby. As he looked on, Toby's wide shoulders expanded on a deep breath before falling again.

"I'm sorry I'm the one you fell in love with."

"I'm not." Even Loyal heard the conviction in his voice.

Toby turned and met Loyal's stare. "Honest to God, I don't know what just happened."

Loyal clasped his hands in his lap. "Apparently, you kissed Mister's ex. An ex he seems to not be the least bit over. I also just learned—alongside almost everyone I know—why the letter I sent you was sitting on the counter the other day."

Toby closed his eyes and turned his face to the sky, as if praying for help. When he met Loyal's stare again, he looked devastated. "I was upset, and Mister showed up to get directions to his appointments. Seriously, baby, I wasn't thinking. I'm so used to being the one who takes care of everyone, I didn't know what to do when I was the one in need. I just needed advice or something. Obviously, I chose the wrong person, but I was desperate. As to kissing Kevin, I have no excuse. We weren't together then, and I was starting to feel like we never would be. I'm so, so fucking sorry. Tell me what to do, because— honestly—I'm starting to wonder if you're not better off without me. Obviously, I have no fucking clue what I'm doing, except screwing up."

Loyal tried hard to cling to his calm. Losing Toby wasn't an option. Loyal wouldn't survive it. "Is that what you want? To be without the burden of me?"

"Stop fucking calling yourself a burden," Toby yelled swiping his hand through the air. "You have never, not for one second, been a burden for me. I love you. I don't want anyone or anything else."

"Then fucking act like it," Loyal growled, feeling his temper slip. "If you love me, stop acting like us being apart is even an option for you. You turned to a friend in your time of need. There's no one to blame for how that turned out other than Mister. Friends don't pull the bullshit he just did. If you want to be mad, be pissed off at him. Don't punish us because of what he did. I'm not. I refuse to let anyone or anything come between us, because —for fuck's sake—I've already almost lost my life to letting things come between us. Aren't you tired of bullshit? I am. I just want to get married and be happy. Can we just do that already, Toby? I'm exhausted."

Toby stared at Loyal like he had lost his mind. Maybe he had. Loyal never yelled. He was the one who kept everything bottled up until it boiled over in the unhealthiest ways. But he was so angry with life for constantly getting in his way, he couldn't contain it anymore. Loyal loved Toby. That was all that mattered to him. He didn't want to fight against it anymore. He was tired. Toby rocked to the side and dug his cellphone out of his back pocket. Loyal watched as he spent a moment clicking around before returning his phone to his pocket as he stood.

"Let's go, sexy."

Loyal dropped his chin and stared at his lap as Toby took control of his chair. Maybe he had worn Toby out a long time ago. Now, he had the option to be free of him and he would. Tanner and Henry were sitting on the back porch when they reached the house. They rolled the basketball between each other, looking adorably in love. Loyal's chest hurt.

"Hey, Henry. Can I call in a favor?" Toby asked the moment they were within earshot.

"Always," Henry answered without missing a beat.

"Great. Are y'all up for a trip to Vegas? Tucker and Orion are meeting us there in the morning."

Tanner chuckled. "You two finally done being dumb, huh?"

Loyal looked between everyone, trying to figure out what the hell was going on.

Toby nodded. "I promised Loyal we would get married and have a nice quiet life. So, that's what we're going to do. I'd love for my brothers to be a part of that, but I understand if you can't."

Tanner stood. "I'll round up Jericho while Henry calls our pilot and you two go pack. Henry and I already have this eloping thing down pat. We'll have you married by tomorrow."

Loyal tried keeping up with the whirlwind that was the Kodiak brothers. Once they decided to do something, everyone else was road debris. The thing was, Toby was taking him to get married. Toby was showing he was serious and ensuring Loyal never had to worry again. They would be settled and happy. Just like Toby promised. Just like Loyal demanded. Guilt washed over Loyal as he followed

Toby into the house and down the hall. He snagged Toby's hand as they reached the bedroom.

"Baby, hold on a second, okay?"

Toby held his stare. He didn't look happy and that hurt Loyal's heart. If Toby didn't really want this, then neither did Loyal.

Loyal tugged at his hand. "Come down here. Take a breath." Toby dropped to his haunches, getting on Loyal's level. Loyal stroked his face. His heart skipped a beat—the way it always did when Loyal really looked at Toby. He was so beautiful. His forest green eyes looked so damn gorgeous, especially locked on Loyal as they were now. "Is this really what you want? Do you want Tucker to leave his honeymoon? Do you want everyone rushing to Vegas in the middle of the night? Do you want me for the rest of your life?"

"Yes." Toby said the word as if he didn't have a single doubt. "Remember what you said about my brothers the other night. We're a team. There's nothing any one of us can do that inconveniences the others. We never thought any of us would be happy, but I found that with you. They want that for us every bit as much as I want you." He handed his phone to Loyal. "Read the texts."

Loyal opened the texts between Tucker and

Toby that Toby had obviously been sending at the dock.

Toby: *Can you meet me in Vegas in the morning?*

Tucker: *Only if I'm getting another brother out of the deal.*

Toby: *Yep.*

Tucker: *Thank fuck. It's about time Loyal joined the family. It's also about damn time you stopped acting like a melon.*

Toby: *What the fuck is that supposed to mean?*

Tucker: *You've been acting like a cantaloupe. Like you cant-elope. LOL!*

Toby: ***groans***

Loyal shook his head. He loved this family. They were completely unique and insane. He was a perfect fit. Loyal's gaze lifted, colliding with Toby's. His eyes burned. "I'm sorry I yelled at you." Even Loyal heard the way his voice cracked.

"I'm not. Maybe it's odd, but I've never felt better about us than I do right now. It seems like everything possible—good and bad—has happened to us this week, but we're both still fighting to be together. You weren't screaming at me. You were yelling *for* me. I think you're fucking perfect."

Loyal had to clear away the lump in his throat to

speak. It still sounded in his voice. "I need a shower before we go."

The wicked glint that entered Toby's eyes at Loyal's words had Loyal's mouth going dry. "I'm sure we have time."

Without a word, Loyal peeled off his shirt. Toby shot forward and claimed Loyal's mouth in a scorching kiss. Loyal clung to Toby's shirt like it was his sanity. Toby lifted Loyal into his arms like he weighed nothing. In a matter of seconds, Loyal went from sitting in his chair and kissing Toby, to beneath him on the bed. Toby leaned away only long enough to whip his shirt over his head and toss it aside before he was back, kissing Loyal deep. The way Toby's muscles bunched and rolled beneath Loyal's hands had Loyal massaging every place he could reach. He wanted to memorize every inch. Soon, in a matter of a few short hours, this would be his husband. Loyal could barely retain his excitement. Everything he had never even dared to dream was within reach. There was so much love suffocating Loyal he didn't know what to do other than to try to make Toby feel it.

He tore at the front of Toby's jeans, ripping open his zipper. Loyal whimpered as Toby's cock filled his hand. He wanted Toby so badly his skin itched.

Loyal tore his mouth away. Desperation ruled him. "Climb up here and put it in my mouth. I want your dick in my mouth." Loyal couldn't stop the plea. He didn't care how he sounded. He ached for Toby.

Toby rolled to the side and jerked off his clothes in frantic motions. He looked every bit as crazed as Loyal felt. Loyal's heart rate didn't slow until Toby straddled his head and traced Loyal's lips with his cock. Loyal opened. His tongue shot out. He swiped Toby's crown with his tongue, teasing. An inhuman sounding growl came from the back of Toby's throat. Loyal's cock dripped pre-cum at the sound. He wrapped his lips around the head of Toby's erection and sucked.

Toby whimpered. "Damn, Loyal. You're killing me."

He was killing himself too. Loyal opened wider, letting Toby's dick scrape the roof of his mouth. Saliva flooded his mouth. Loyal sucked. He fought the urge to palm his cock. He was so damn horny. Loyal could barely stand it. He squeezed the globes of Toby's ass and rocked him forward as he sucked again, treating him like a lollipop.

Toby pulled away. "I'm sorry, sexy. I'm too far gone." That was all the warning Loyal got before he found himself nude, lubed, and filled with hard cock.

Toby slammed upward, over and over again without mercy. His tongue fought with Loyal's, keeping his mouth busy as he pounded Loyal's ass. There was no mercy. No slow build. Loyal got fucked and his orgasm hit with almost no warning. Loyal cried out around Toby's tongue and tore at the skin of Toby's back, scratching for purchase like it was his sanity. Cum molded their bodies together.

Toby tore his mouth away and roared as he came. It was the sexiest sound Loyal had ever heard. As his high abated, a new reality settled in. They couldn't be broken. No matter what happened. No matter how huge of an obstacle that tried shoving between them, they always ended up right here—joined as one. Toby and Loyal were always loyal to each other's love. They always would be, because they had chosen each other.

EIGHT

SIX WEEKS of married life had proven one thing to Toby above everything else—he was right where he was supposed to be. Beyond spending two days in Vegas, they hadn't gotten a honeymoon. For now, Loyal's therapy came first. He couldn't afford to lose any of the progress he had made. Loyal got stronger every day. It was humbling to watch him fight. Toby had never been prouder of anyone in his life.

"Five more steps unassisted and I'll stop for ice cream on the way home."

Loyal held the bars on either side of him and huffed. "It's February. It's fifty-two outside."

Toby's eyebrows rose. "Are you saying you don't want ice cream?"

A childish sounding sniff escaped Loyal. He

mumbled like a kid. "I'm not saying I don't want ice cream."

Loyal's physical therapist, Abby, bit her bottom lip, hiding a smile.

Toby didn't let up. "Then let go of those rails and take five more steps toward me."

Loyal's chest expanded on a deep breath. His shoulders rose and fell. He let go of the bars. Toby released a breath he hadn't known he was holding when Loyal didn't fall. It always jammed Toby's heart into his throat every time Loyal went down. His bruises were Toby's. Loyal's disappointments weighed a lot on Toby's shoulders. They were a team. Loyal took three steps. Toby was back to holding his breath. By the fourth step, Loyal's entire body shook from the effort. Toby tried shifting his rolling chair closer on the sly. He didn't want Loyal to give up, but he also didn't want him to get hurt. On the fifth step, Loyal's knees collapsed but Toby was there. He snagged Loyal's waist and pulled him into his lap. Toby cheered, smoothing over any awkwardness.

"Woot. That was awesome, baby." Loyal beamed beneath Toby's pride. Toby kissed him hard and loud before pulling away. "You're so amazing. Pretty soon you won't need me at all. Now, let's grab your chair so you can get some water." Toby helped Loyal into his chair and stole another kiss.

"I love you," Loyal whispered before wheeling away to grab some water. Toby watched his every move with love crushing his windpipe. It never got old, knowing Loyal was his.

"You're great with him," Abby said, wiping down the bars. "I wish every one of my patients came with a spouse like you. Loyal probably wouldn't have come half as far without you."

Toby shrugged, uncomfortable with the praise. "We're a team. He would do the same for me, if the shoe was on the other foot."

As Toby watched Loyal across the room, he recognized that was why he had never let go. Never moved on. Never gave up hope. Possibly there was someone else on the planet who would always come through for Toby the way Loyal did, but he doubted it. He definitely had no desire to search for someone else, knowing full well no one was Loyal's equal. Eventually everyone had to choose what came first in life. Loyal never let Toby forget he was that thing Loyal had chosen in the world. For Toby, it would always be Loyal. For the rest of their lives, it would always be them.

KEVIN WISHED HE COULD SAY HE WAS SURPRISED to see Haven. As Kevin opened his front door to find Haven standing on his front porch, he realized he wasn't shocked in the least. Haven always showed up when Kevin decided he was the most done with him.

"Haven." Even Kevin heard the hatred in his voice.

His wicked lips lifted in one corner. "That's not what you used to call me."

A growl rose in Kevin's throat. "Well, I also used to wet the bed as a kid and call my sister every night before she died. Things change."

Haven's blue gaze skirted away. His smirk disappeared. "May I come in?"

Kevin wanted to say no, but he equally didn't want his neighbors talking. Ever since Haven started doing those stupid BDSM demos for the rich, everyone knew his face. Unfortunately, almost everyone also knew they used to date. There was nothing quite like having everyone debate his sexual behaviors, wondering if Haven practiced what he preached with Kevin. He did, or he had. That was no one's business.

Kevin took a step back, letting Haven inside.

"What do you want?" He didn't try sugarcoating things. Haven wouldn't be here if he didn't want something, and there wasn't a damn thing Kevin could imagine giving him, except maybe a black eye. He fought an evil grin at the thought.

"Since I can see you're already picturing me being disemboweled, I promise I won't stay long." Damn. His face must have given him away after all.

"That's probably best."

Haven gave him a short nod. He didn't move to sit or take off his jacket. It was obvious he intended to say what he came to say and then go. "Toby's husband Loyal gave me some great advice after the last time I saw you. Actually, it was more of a kick in the pants than advice, but still. And now, Orion isn't speaking to me. I never realized how much that would hurt." He took a breath, as if realizing he was half a second away from rambling. Haven held his gaze. "I'm sorry. This isn't an I'm sorry, please take me back. I'm genuinely really, really sorry for everything I did." The backs of Kevin's eyes burned. His throat swelled. He didn't want to hear this apology. All Kevin wanted was for Haven to disappear and maybe for the rumor to reach him later that Haven's dick had fallen off. Kevin didn't ask for much. But Haven wasn't done talking. "You deserve so much better than you got from me. I took advantage of your heart. Worse than that, I abused your trust. I'm not asking for your forgiveness. I know I'm beyond that. The only reason I'm here is because I need you to know that I fully recognize what I did wrong and what I lost because of it." Haven paused and visibly swallowed. It hit Kevin. He was hurting. Kevin never would have believed it if he wasn't seeing it with his own eyes. Haven cleared his throat. "I hope you find the happiness you deserve and never think of me again."

Without looking back, Haven headed for the door. Confusion scattered Kevin's thoughts, leaving him torn. He had loved this man once upon a time with every fiber of his being. Sometimes, the magnitude of what he lost would slam down on him in the most unexpected moments and crush the air from his lungs. But, at the end of the day, it was himself he could never forgive. "Mister." Haven froze with his hand on the knob. His gaze shot Kevin's way at the name. Kevin swallowed. It hurt to see Haven's face more than words could describe. "Don't come back here."

At Kevin's words, Haven gave him a sharp nod and let himself out. He had no idea how much time passed as he stared at the spot where Haven had been. Strong arms encircled his waist, pulling him back against a solid chest. Warm lips brushed his neck, making goosebumps rise on his skin.

"Are you okay, gorgeous?"

Kevin reached over his shoulder and ran his fingers through Jericho's hair, holding him in place. The tightness eased in his chest. "Yeah. I'm good."

Jericho's lips moved to Kevin's shoulder. "Good. You should come back to bed."

Yes. He should. Kevin was done with Haven. He wouldn't waste another day on what might have been.

KEEP AN EYE OUT FOR THE NEXT CUBS FOR Rent, *Before Him*.

Please consider leaving a review at the retailer where this book was purchased. Reviews really help with a book's visibility, which ensures I can continue writing. Thank you, Charity.

ABOUT THE AUTHOR

Charity Parkerson is an award winning and multi-published author with several companies. Born with no filter from her brain to her mouth, she decided to take this odd quirk and insert it in her characters.

*Eight-time Readers' Favorite Award Winner
    *2015 Passionate Plume Award Finalist
    *2013 Reviewers' Choice Award Winner
    *2012 ARRA Finalist for Favorite Paranormal Romance
    *Five-time winner of The Mistress of the Darkpath

Connect with her online:

--Join my street team: facebook.com/TeamCharityParkerson
    --Website: charityparkerson.com
    --Facebook: facebook.com/authorCharityParkerson

facebook.com/TheMenofSin

--Twitter: twitter.com/CharityParkerso